THE
Empty Box
AND
Zeroth
Maria
1

Eiji Mikage

ILLUSTRATION BY 415

March 2—the day when everything normal in my life as Kazuki Hoshino *shatters*. It starts with a transfer student, Aya Otonashi.

"I'm Aya Otonashi.

"—Kazuki Hoshino.
I'm here to break you."

Her enmity
toward me is
palpable...Why?
Why me, of
all people?

Kazuki Hoshino
A perfectly average first-year high school student in Class 6. His favorite food is Umaibo snacks. Aya, a total stranger, has sworn she will break him.

AYA
OTONASHI

Aya Otonashi
A transfer student who
arrives on the odd date of
March 2—almost the end
of the school year—only
to suddenly declare in
front of the entire class
her intent to break the
"culprit" Kazuki.

March 2—Homeroom

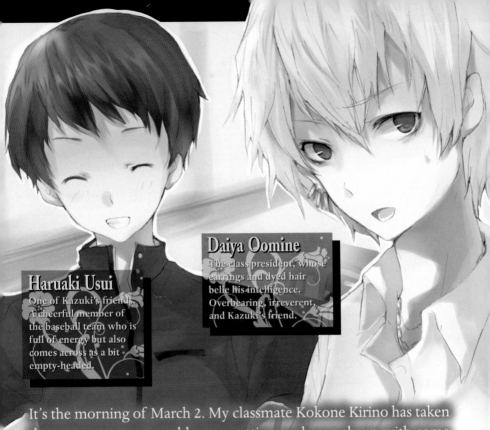

Haruaki Usui
One of Kazuki's friends.
A cheerful member of
the baseball team who is
full of energy but also
comes across as a bit
empty-headed.

Daiya Oomine
The class president, whose
earrings and dyed hair
belie his intelligence.
Overbearing, irreverent,
and Kazuki's friend.

It's the morning of March 2. My classmate Kokone Kirino has taken the seat next to me and begun putting on her makeup with some tool I have no idea what to call.

"Do you notice anything different about me today? Anything at all?"

Despite her asking, I can't see what would have changed. I can't tell what she wants me to notice. How am I supposed to figure that out?

"Don't just butt in, Kiri."

"You're the same as ever."

And with that, Daiya and Kokone begin their usual rapid-fire exchange. They've both got mouths on them, that's for sure...

Kokone Kirino
Kazuki's upbeat and sociable classmate who can also be a bit of a busybody. Her friendship with Daiya Oomine dates back to kindergarten.

March 2—Before Class

Kasumi Mogi

Kazuki's delicate and silent classmate who is also the object of his affection. She is the most frequent victim of the March 3 incident.

It's the morning of March 3.
I'm at an intersection with poor visibility
due to the rain. This is where *that* will take
place—an unavoidable, unstoppable thing
bound to happen no matter what.

That is what made me take action.
It's the reason I fight and
why I've taken a stand.
All because the person I am now
has sworn never to give up...

"N-nooo!"

March 3—Morning

There we are, within the soft,

pure-white sweetness of despair.

Designed by Toru Suzuki

THE

Empty Box

AND

Zeroth Maria

1

EIJI MIKAGE

ILLUSTRATION BY 415

New York

The Empty Box and Zeroth Maria, Vol. 1
Eiji Mikage

Translation by Luke Baker
Cover art by 415

UTSURO NO HAKO TO ZERO NO MARIA Vol. 1
Edited by ASCII MEDIA WORKS
First published in Japan in 2009 by KADOKAWA CORPORATION, Tokyo.
English translation rights arranged with KADOKAWA CORPORATION, Tokyo through
TUTTLE-MORI AGENCY, INC., Tokyo.

Yen On
1290 Avenue of the Americas
New York, NY 10104

Visit us at yenpress.com
facebook.com/yenpress
twitter.com/yenpress
yenpress.tumblr.com
instagram.com/yenpress

First Yen On Edition: October 2017

Yen On is an imprint of Yen Press, LLC.
The Yen On name and logo are trademarks of Yen Press, LLC.

Library of Congress Cataloging-in-Publication Data
Names: Mikage, Eiji author. | 415, illustrator. | Baker, Luke, translator.
Title: The empty box and zeroth Maria / Eiji Mikage ; illustration by 415 ;
translation by Luke Baker.
Other titles: Utsuro no Hako to Zero no Maria. English
Description: First Yen On edition. | New York, NY : Yen On, 2017.
Identifiers: LCCN 2017027929 | ISBN 9780316561105 (v. 1 : paperback)
Subjects: | CYAC: Science fiction. | BISAC: FICTION / Science Fiction / General.
Classification: LCC PZ7.1.M553 Em 2017 | DDC [Fic]—dc23
LC record available at https://lccn.loc.gov/2017027929

ISBNs: 978-0-316-56110-5 (paperback)
978-0-316-56123-5 (ebook)

1 3 5 7 9 10 8 6 4 2

LSC-C

Printed in the United States of America

It's not like I've forgotten. I'm pretty sure I remember where this place is, and I've actually seen this scenery in my dreams.

However, outside of those dreams, I can't recall what it looks like.

But it's not like I forgot. Not at all. It's just that I don't have the proper cue I need to draw the memory out. Reality offers me no opportunities to remember. I'm sure if I did try to recall it, if I even can, then I wouldn't get the chance to do so.

I mean, the person standing before me now has absolutely *no connection* to the reality I know.

"Do you have a wish?"

The face of the man (woman?) asking me this in such placid tones keeps changing, never staying the same for long. The deepest parts of my psyche that weave this dream can't seem to pin down its features. I'm sure I've seen this face somewhere before. It simultaneously resembles everyone and no one.

My answer must have been bland and noncommittal. That's why I can't remember the response I receive. But the person listens to my reply all the same and then hands me some sort of container.

"This Box can grant any wish, no matter what it may be."

It really does look like a box.

I squint my eyes as I examine it more closely. My vision isn't poor.

Despite this, I still can't seem to see the Box clearly, even though it's so close. It's empty.

And something seems very wrong about that. It's like shaking an unopened box of cookies where you can feel the weight of the contents and hear them rattling around, only to find it's empty when you open it.

I'm sure the next thing I did was ask some boring question like "Why are you giving this to me?"

"Because you're so very interesting. You're all so similar that I find it practically impossible to see the little things that distinguish you. You intrigue me to no end, yet I simply can't tell one of you from another. It's all very ironic."

I have no idea what this means, but I nod as if I do.

"I can identify you, though. You might not think much of it, but that's more than enough to catch my eye."

I look inside at the bottom of the Box. Though there isn't anything in there, I feel myself overcome by the uncomfortable sensation that something is trying to pull me within. I quickly avert my gaze.

"Use this Box, and whatever wish you could possibly have will come true. It doesn't matter what you ask for. You could wish eternal sorrow upon the entire human race, and I wouldn't lift a finger to stop you. All I want is to see what kind of wishes you, all of you, will make."

Whatever I say next brings a smile to the other person's face.

"Heh-heh… No, no, it's not some sort of special power. It's actually the innate ability of humans to possess clearly defined visions that makes their wishes come true. All I can do is give that ability a little push."

I take the Box. But of course, I don't remember that, or this dream, once I wake up.

I can still clearly recall how I felt about that man, and my impression never changes, even within the dream.

This guy's…

…kinda creepy, isn't he?

1st Time
Otonashi
23rd Time
4,609th Time
1,050th Time
8,946th Time

5,232nd Time

10,876th Time

27,753rd Time

27,753rd Time

2,602nd Time

2,601st Time

13,118th Time

Aya

1st Time

"My name is Aya Otonashi. I'm very pleased to meet you," the transfer student said with a small smile.

23rd Time

"I'm Aya Otonashi… Nice to meet you," the transfer student said, her voice uninterested and emotionless.

1,050th Time

"I'm Aya Otonashi," the transfer student spat, sounding jaded and refusing to meet the gazes of her new classmates.

13,118th Time

I look at the platform in the front of the classroom and see a new transfer student named Aya Otonashi, *whose name I've never learned*. "I'm Aya Otonashi" is the only thing she mumbles as she faces her schoolmates.

Her voice is so quiet, it's as if she doesn't care if anyone can hear her. All the same, her clear tones carry well.

—Yeah. I know her name. But of course, *this is the first time I've actually heard it.*

The class can scarcely breathe. Not because her curt self-introduction could barely be called a greeting, but because there's something unearthly about this girl and her matchless beauty.

Everyone is waiting to hear what she'll say next. The girl opens her mouth.

"Kazuki Hoshino."

"...Huh?"

Why did she say my name? Every gaze in the classroom settles on me as if I'm going to tell them why. They can look at me all they want, but I'm just as clueless as they are.

"I'm here to break you," the girl says suddenly. "This is the 13,118th time I've transferred. After so many occasions, I have to say that this is all starting to grate on me, which is why this time I'm spicing things up with a proper declaration of war."

She fixates on me, unconcerned by the blank astonishment gripping the rest of the class.

"Kazuki Hoshino, I will make you surrender. It would be best if you offered what you value most to me immediately. There's no point in resisting. Why, you ask? The answer is simple..."

Aya Otonashi's lips curl into a smile as she continues.

"No matter how much time passes, I will always be right there with you."

10,876th Time

It's March 2. Today has to be March 2.

Why do I need to remind myself of that?

...Must be because it's still so cloudy outside despite it being March.

That's got to be it. It's the weather, the way the blue sky remains hidden just enough to dampen your spirits.

When the hell is it ever going to clear up?

I'm in the classroom before the bell rings, and those are the kinds of dull thoughts going through my mind as I stare out the window.

I'm sure I'm only thinking this way because something's off with me. I mean, not that I'm sick. I feel the same as ever. There's just something...weird about me today.

I can't really describe it, but I guess it's closer to a sense of wrongness, like suddenly noticing I'm the only one not casting a shadow.

...It's so bizarre that I can't put my finger on the cause. It's not like anything special happened yesterday. This morning I ate breakfast and listened to a new album by one of my favorite bands on the train, and when I happened to catch my horoscope for the day on TV, it said I would have passably good luck.

Anyway, it's not like dwelling on it will uncover any answers, so I might as well eat my Umaibo. Today's flavor is pork kimchi. I take a bite of the crispy puffed-corn stick. No matter how many of these I eat, I'll never get tired of that texture.

"Umaibo again? Don't you ever get sick of those things? If you keep eating them every day like this, your blood will probably turn the same color."

"...Um, what color would that be?"

"You think I care?"

The one responsible for this nonsense is my classmate Kokone Kirino. Her brown hair, which falls somewhere between semilong and long, is tied back in a single high ponytail. Kokone changes how she does her hair all the time, but this style seems to be a favorite of hers lately. It feels like I haven't seen her do it any other way for a while.

Kokone takes the seat next me and peers into a light-blue hand mirror as she does her makeup with some tool a guy like me has no idea what to call.

She's so focused, it almost makes me want to tell her to try concentrating that hard on something other than cosmetics.

"Now that I think about it, a lot of your things are blue."

"Um, yeah, that's because I like it. Oh yeah, Kazu, do you notice anything different about me today? Anything at all?"

With that abrupt change of topic, Kokone turns to face me, her eyes glittering.

"Hmm...?"

What could it be? How am I supposed to know if she just asks me without warning like that?

"Here's a hint! Something has changed about my most attractive feature!"

"Huh?"

I look at her chest without thinking.

"Hey! What, you think it's my breasts?!"

Can I help it if Kokone is always bragging about how she outgrew her D cups?

"Everyone knows my most striking feature is my big, beautiful eyes. As if my breasts could just get bigger overnight! Or maybe that's what you were hoping, you perv! You're obsessed with boobs!"

"...Sorry."

I had no way of knowing what Kokone considers her "most attractive feature," but I figure it's best to just apologize.

"...So? What do you think?"

Kokone gazes directly at me, her eyes brimming with expectation. They certainly are big. Now that I realize it, I can't help but feel a bit embarrassed.

"......But your face looks the same as usual."

I try not to stare too closely at her face as I say this.

"What's that? You say my face is as lovely as always?"

"That's not what I said!"

"Well, you should!" she demands. "I'll have you know that I'm using mascara today. How is it? What do you think?"

I still can't tell what she wants me to notice. She looks exactly the same as yesterday.

"......I mean, how am I supposed to notice that?"

I was going for the honest approach, but it was the wrong choice.

"What do you mean...'How am I supposed to notice that?'?!"

Kokone hits me.

"Ow..."

"Ugh! Could you possibly be any more boring?!"

Kokone sounds like she's just playing around, but I think I'm detecting a hint of genuine anger in her voice.

She pretends to spit on the floor and goes to show off her new mascara look to the rest of the class.

"Phew..."

That really wore me out. Kokone is fun, but I can't keep up with her.

"You two lovebirds finished with your little spat?"

The first thing I see upon turning around is a right ear with three earrings in it. There's only one person in our school with those...

"...Daiya, there's no way anyone could mistake that for a lover's quarrel. That would've happened no matter what."

But my friend Daiya Oomine blows off my rebuttal with a snort. Yep, he's just as arrogant as ever today. But I guess it would be pretty weird if someone decked themselves out with silver hair and tons of accessories, blatantly violating school rules, only to act all meek and humble.

"Could you seriously not tell she had mascara on? I couldn't care less about how she looks, and even I could see the difference."

"......Really?"

Daiya lives next door to Kokone and has apparently known her since kindergarten, so his claim that he doesn't care about her has to be a lie. Still, I might have a problem if I missed something even this self-centered and dismissive guy picked up on.

"...But, you know..."

I feel like she was wearing mascara yesterday, too.

"Oh, I got you, Kazu. You're just letting that ho know you aren't into her. I feel you there. I do the same thing, only I'm more upfront about it."

"You're such a jackass for a class president! I can hear everything you're saying, you know!"

Daiya continues on, completely ignoring Kokone and her infamously sharp ears. "Enough about all that, though. Have you heard there's a new student transferring to our class today?"

"A transfer student?"

I confirm with myself again that it's March 2. Why would anyone transfer so late in the school year?

"A transfer student! Really?!" Kokone really was listening in the whole time, evident by her jumping in now.

"I'm not talking to you, Kiri. Don't just butt in from across the room. And don't try to come over here, either. For the sake of my mental health, I don't want to look at that sloppy paint job you're so hell-bent on applying to your face."

"Wh-what?! Well, maybe you should think about doing something to fix that messed up attitude of yours first, Daiya! Go hang upside down for forty-six hours, and maybe you might get some blood flow to your head again so you can start using it!"

They've both got mouths on them, that's for sure. I raise my voice to speak over them, trying to put an end to the trash talking and steer the conversation back on topic.

"So, a transfer student? I think I may have heard something about that."

Just as I planned, Daiya shuts his mouth and gives me a long stare.

"...And who'd you hear that from?" he asks me, a serious expression on his face.

"Huh? Why does that matter?"

"Don't answer my question with a question."

"Um... Who told me, again? I think it might have been you."

"That's impossible. I heard about the transfer student myself only just now when I went to the faculty room on an errand. There's no way I would've had time to tell you."

"You're sure?"

"Rumors about this type of thing spread like wildfire. Kiri is about the biggest gossip out there, and even she was clueless."

Thinking back on what I just witnessed, I realize he's right. In fact, none of our classmates in first-year Class 6 seem to be in the know.

"That means they kept the information under wraps until today, the actual day of the transfer. If that's the case, then why would you know about it?"

"...Ummm, I don't know."

I wonder why?

"I guess it really doesn't matter. But still, don't you think it's a bit odd, Kazu? Why would we have a transfer student arriving so late in the year? The way I see it, something must have happened. Maybe she's a real problem child, like the daughter of some chairman who got kicked out of another school. That's a believable reason for transferring now and keeping the news on the down-low."

"You shouldn't make crazy speculations and form a biased opinion of the girl before she even arrives, Daiya! Transfer students have enough trouble with people thinking weird things about them as it is. Not to mention that everyone's eavesdropping." Kokone's reprimand provokes some wry grins from the classmates who were indeed listening in.

"So? You think I care?"

Wow...

Just as a reflexive sigh escapes me at Daiya's overbearing attitude, the bell rings.

The rest of the class gradually makes their way to their seats.

Kokone is sitting in the row closest to the hallway, so she opens the hall window and leans out over the sill.

It seems she wants to be the first to see our new classmate.

"Oh!" she blurts out, as if she's spotted someone who fits the bill.

Apparently, she's having fun getting an eyeful, but then she suddenly lets out a yelp and returns to her seat with a wooden expression on her face.

What could have happened?

A smile rises on Kokone's face as she whispers, "Wow."

I'm sure I'm not the only one who wants to ask her what she saw, but without a moment's notice, our teacher, Mr. Kokubo, enters the classroom.

The shadow of a female student appears behind the frosted glass on the door.

Observing the classroom and noticing everyone's curiosity, Mr. Kokubo calls in the transfer student.

The silhouette on the other side of the door moves.

And that's when I see her...

It's instantaneous.

The entire scene changes, as if the classroom itself has just been hurled off a cliff.

The first thing I notice is a particular sound.

It's a dry scratching noise, a rasping sound like our surroundings are being ripped apart.

Scene after scene violently and forcefully interposes.

Similar sights appear over and over.

My mind runs wild, only to find itself forced back and tightly locked in place, like it's being crammed into a little metal box.

"My name is Aya Otonashi," I hear.

"I'm Aya Otonashi," I hear.

"I'm Aya Otonashi." *I heard you, dammit!*

I reject those words against the massive tide of information trying to force itself into my head. There's no room for anything else. My brain is going to be sick. There's no way it can possibly digest all of this.

"Ah…"

I…

What…? I can't understand any of this.

Once I realize this, I shut my thoughts away…and I'm back to normal.

Huh? What was I thinking about just now?

I've forgotten, so I turn back toward the front of the classroom and look at her.

At the transfer student, Aya Otonashi, *whose name I have yet to learn.*

"I'm Aya Otonashi" is the only thing she mumbles, in a voice that seems to imply she couldn't care less if we heard her or not.

She steps down from the podium.

The entire class is buzzing at her terse self-introduction.

She starts walking toward me, apparently oblivious to the confusion of her new classmates.

Gazing directly at me.

She matter-of-factly takes the seat next to me, which just happens to be empty, *almost as if it were set aside specifically for her to sit in.*

Otonashi has been examining me with undisguised suspicion as I watched all this transpire in stunned silence.

…Maybe I should say something.

"……Um, nice to meet you."

But her scowl remains unchanged.

"Is that it?"

"Huh…?"

"I asked you if that's it."

Am I missing something? I can't think of what she could possibly mean. This is the first time in my life I've ever seen Aya Otonashi.

But the mood in the air suggests there's something else I need to say.

"……Uh, is that uniform from your old school?"

My forced question elicits no reaction from Otonashi, who continues to stare at me.

"…Okay?"

Seeing my bewilderment, Otonashi sighs for some reason, and her lips turn up in the kind of exasperated smile you use with a disobedient child.

"I'll let you in on a secret you might like, Hoshino."

…Huh? I don't recall telling her my name.

That's the least of the surprises in store for me, though.

Five seconds later, Otonashi's next utterance stuns me into silence.

"Kasumi Mogi is wearing light-blue panties today."

Kasumi Mogi generally wears her regular school uniform during PE instead of her gym clothes. Today is no different. She's wearing her usual uniform while she watches the boys play soccer, her expression as lifeless as some sort of doll. The pale legs extending from below her skirt are so slender it seems as if they could break at any moment.

And for some reason, I'm resting my head on those legs.

Okay, yeah. At this point, I officially give up trying to understand any of this. I'm happy, but my brain isn't ready to process the situation. All I can do is put the tissue to my nose and focus on stopping the bleeding. I think I might lose my mind if I don't.

I more or less understand how this situation came about. I couldn't focus because of Otonashi, and so the soccer ball hit me in the face and gave me a bloody nose. Mogi was worried about me and, for some reason, let me rest my head on her lap.

Her legs aren't soft at all, though. To be honest, they kinda hurt my head.

Why is she doing this?

I look up at her, but her expression is blank and unreadable.

Still, I'm happy.

I'm hopelessly and helplessly happy.

Of course Otonashi's revelation about the panties startled me, but not just because of how sudden it was. Like, she said she would tell me a secret I "might like." She knew that information about Kasumi Mogi would qualify, and that's what really caught me off guard.

Not even Daiya or Kokone is aware of my love for Mogi.

Why would Otonashi, someone I supposedly just met today, have any clue about my feelings?

And yet she still said what she said.

"...Hey, Mogi..."

"What?" she replies in a soft voice, like a small bird's. It suits her petite frame and delicate appearance perfectly.

"Did Otonashi talk to you at all today?"

"Otonashi, the transfer student? ...No."

"So you aren't friends with her at all?"

Mogi shakes her head no.

"Has anything strange happened to you recently?"

After thinking a moment, Mogi responds the same way, and the soft waves of her hair sway along with her.

"Why do you ask...?" she replies, her head tilted to one side.

"Ah, well...no reason."

Looking over toward the playing field, I see Otonashi standing in the center like a statue, utterly uninterested in the ball and the group of girls swarming around it. When it happens to roll over to her, she kicks it back to another player, who appears to be on the other team.

"Hmm..."

Maybe I'm overthinking things. Maybe she doesn't really know how I feel.

Otonashi's appearance, or even just her attitude, really makes an impression.

When someone like her suddenly makes that kind of declaration from earlier, I can't help but read too much into it, right? Perfectly understandable.

Still, why do I have so much trouble believing it?

Otonashi looks in my direction.

And her gaze stays locked onto me.

The corner of her mouth lifting defiantly, she starts marching in my direction, even though class isn't finished yet.

I quickly find myself on my feet.

Though it should have been the greatest happiness of my life, I've relinquished the right to rest my head on Mogi's legs.

I'm shivering from head to toe.

And I don't mean that as a mere figure of speech—my entire body really is shaking.

Perhaps because she's noticed Otonashi approaching, Mogi also rises to her feet, her face taut with unease.

Otonashi walks up to me, that same defiant smirk still on her face... and suddenly jabs her finger at Mogi.

It's all very abrupt.

There's a sudden gust of wind. With absolutely no forewarning whatsoever. That no one could have predicted.

And that breeze lifts Mogi's skirt.

"~~~~!!"

Mogi quickly grabs the hem to hold it in place—only the front, though, and I'm standing behind her.

The wind is gone as suddenly as it arrived, and Mogi looks back at me. Though her face is as blank as ever, her cheeks are just the slightest bit red. She mouths the words "Did you see?" Or maybe she says them in a voice too quiet to hear. I shake my head *no* with all my might, though I'm sure the vehemence of my denial gives it away that I'm lying. But all Mogi does is lower her gaze without another word.

Otonashi quickly appears beside me.

I catch a glimpse of her expression.

"Uhhh—"

It's then I learn the reason why I'm trembling. I can read what's behind that look. It's something I've never once had directed toward me in my entire life: enmity.

Why? Why me of all people?

Otonashi's still glaring at me with that sneer. As I stand there, unable to do anything but shiver, she places her hand on my shoulder and brings her lips to my ear.

"They were light blue, right?"

Otonashi knew everything. That I have feelings for Mogi, that a gust of wind would reveal Mogi's underwear in front of me—everything, from start to finish.

What she said to me earlier wasn't just some joke.

It was a threat, meant to insinuate that she understood me, that she knew me inside and out, and that she controlled me.

"Surely *you remember* now, Hoshino?"

She watches my rigid form carefully.

We stand like that for a while, but perhaps dismayed by my lack of response, Otonashi eventually lowers her gaze and lets out a sigh.

"I thought surely that would work... You're even more dim-witted than usual today," she complains in a low voice. "If you've forgotten, then you better remember this. My name is Maria."

Maria? But I thought your name was Aya Otonashi.

"I-is that your pen name or something?"

"Shut up." She doesn't even try to hide her anger. "Fine. You might not be responding, but I'm still going to do what I have to."

And with that, Otonashi turns away.

"Hey, wait..."

I call out for her to stop. She turns around, obviously annoyed.

I instinctively recoil at the sight of her brows furrowed in such anger.

It doesn't makes sense. But judging by her behavior, maybe...

"Is this because we've met somewhere before?"

My question brings a smirk to Otonashi's face.

"Yeah, we were lovers in a former life. My beloved Hathaway, how it pains me to see you reduced to this. To think the man who came to spirit away a princess of an enemy kingdom such as myself could become such a cretin."

"...Uh, I don't think I..."

I'm completely dumbfounded. Perhaps satisfied with my reaction, for the first time today I see what could be a considered a real smile on Otonashi's face.

"Just joking."

The next day, I find Aya Otonashi's lifeless body.

The 8,946th Time

After considering my words for some time with obvious sorrow, Mogi answered in a truly pained voice, "Wait until tomorrow."

The 2,601st Time

"I'm Aya Otonashi."

The transfer student muttered that and nothing more.

"Oh man! This is incredible!"

Haruaki Usui, my friend *in the seat next to me*, blurts this out in a fairly loud voice and gives me an audible slap on the back, even though we're still in the middle of second period.

That hurts, stupid. It's embarrassing, too. Everyone is staring.

Haruaki's gawking behind him thanks to the presence of Aya Otonashi, the transfer student.

"Our eyes met! Oh man, I can't believe this!"

"She probably just looked up when you made all that fuss turning around to look at her."

"Hosshi, my man, you have no sense of romance."

Romance? What the hell's he talking about?

"She's just too beautiful! Like a walking work of art. She's a national treasure. I can't take it anymore! My heart is hers! I'm going to profess my love to her."

Well, that was fast!

The bell rings. Upon giving the end-of-class salute as ordered, Haruaki makes a beeline for Otonashi without even returning to his seat.

"Aya Otonashi! You have stolen my heart. I love you!"

Oh god, he actually went through with it!

I can't hear Otonashi's reply, but I know the outcome right away from Haruaki's face. Actually, I'm pretty sure I didn't even need to see that to deduce her reply.

Haruaki comes back to my desk.

"I can't believe it... She turned me down."

Why did you even think you had a chance of success in the first place? His total sincerity is a bit scary.

"Of course she did. If you go up to someone and announce your love for them unexpectedly like that, they're going to get creeped out. That's just how it works."

"Hmph. Yeah, I guess you're right. I'll just have to try again, only next time it won't be so sudden. I know I'll win her over someday."

While on the one hand I envy Haruaki for his optimism, on the other, I'm glad I'm lacking in that area.

"And what are you two up to here? It seems like fun to me, but the girls sure don't think much of you right now," says Daiya as he walks up to us.

"What?! Just Haruaki, right?"

"Afraid not. They're treating you two as partners in crime."

"Hey, hey, my partner in crime? That's some high praise right there, huh, Hosshi!"

Th-this can't get any worse...

"But how about it, Daiyan? I'm sure even you want to take a shot at her, right?" Haruaki says, giving him a little jab with his elbow.

Most people would be afraid to tease Daiya like this, but Haruaki doesn't give it a second thought, maybe because they're old friends, or maybe because he's not the type to worry about consequences.

Daiya sighs and answers straightaway.

"Nah."

"No way! So does that mean you have your heart set on someone else?"

"It doesn't matter whether Otonashi's good looks stir my heart or not. I'll admit, she is beautiful, but I'd never actually try to make a play for her."

"Hmm, really…?"

"You don't understand anything, do you, Haruaki? But I guess that sentiment is incomprehensible to an ape like you who's driven solely by instinct and pursues anything with a pretty face."

"What'd you say? Just what does caring about looks have to do with instincts?!"

"Producing attractive children will lead to more descendants, so we are instinctively drawn to more visually appealing mates."

"Ohhh," Haruaki and I both say in wonderment. Daiya seems truly disheartened that we never figured this out on our own.

"Phew. Well, I get it, Daiyan. What you're really trying to say is that there's no point in trying because Aya is out of your league, right? There's no dishonor in knowing you can't win! I know what you're doing. You're like that fox that knows he can't reach the grapes high up on the tree, so he tries to make everyone else think those grapes are bitter. Rationalization, that's it. That's so not cool. Laaame, Daiyan!"

"Did you even listen to a word I said? Still, the first part of your argument wasn't completely off base. You should die a thousand times for the second half, though."

"Ha! So you admit you don't have a chance!"

That's enough for Daiya to slug Haruaki and his triumphant grin. *Wow, all that anger he was holding back really boiled to the surface.*

"It's not that I don't have a chance. It's that she won't try to approach me."

"Man, if that isn't some conceited BS, I don't know what is. Right, Hosshi? This guy thinks he deserves the world on a platter just 'cause he's pretty."

You'd think Haruaki would've learned his lesson by now, but he plunges ahead full tilt.

"I'm not saying she won't make a move on me because I'm out of her league. It may be the truth, but that's not how things work with her."

"Damn, you really are shameless!"

"She doesn't think of me as out of her league," Daiya explains. "In fact, I don't even fall into that category for her. None of us interest her one bit. It's not like she's looking down on us, either. It's just like how we see insects only as insects, or people as people. She isn't even aware of the subtle difference between us, how I'm handsome and Haruaki's a total mess. It's like ignoring the differences between male and female cockroaches to her. Just how would you go about making a move on someone who views you like that?"

Not even Haruaki has a clue of what to say in response to this rather merciless criticism of Otonashi.

"...Daiya."

I just have to open my mouth.

"You're actually pretty interested in Otonashi, aren't you?"

Daiya's at a loss for words. A rare reaction for him. But that's the way it is. Regardless of whether his opinions are right or wrong, you can't really analyze them without a bit of observation.

"...Psh, I don't give a damn about her."

"You're blushing."

"...Kazu, you are this close to falling into my trap. I'm going to do things you never thought possible with a green onion that will make you break out in hives the next time you even see one."

I can tell that Daiya is getting seriously angry, so I decide to laugh and play the whole thing off as a joke.

At any rate, it seems that Daiya knows that Otonashi is easy to deal with.

"Before long, even you idiots and your insect-level powers of observation will figure out that there's something wrong with her."

The claim makes Daiya sound like a bit of a sore loser.

But that isn't the case.

After all, he's exactly right.

Immediately after our homeroom session at the end of the day, Otonashi suddenly raises her hand. As soon as Mr. Kokubo sees her, she launches into an announcement without waiting for permission or even an acknowledgment.

"I need everyone in first-year Class 6 to do something."

Heedless of the class's stunned reaction, she continues.

"I just need five minutes of your time. I'm sure you don't mind, right?"

Despite the lack of response, Otonashi marches up to the podium.

She then drives Mr. Kokubo out of the classroom as if it's the most natural thing in the world. The whole scene is bizarre, but for some reason it feels completely normal. Judging by their reactions, I can tell the rest of the class probably feels the same way.

Pure silence grips the classroom, without a single murmur of protest.

Standing on the platform at the front, Otonashi faces the class and opens her mouth to speak.

"I want you all to write something."

She then steps down and gives piles of something to the students at the front of each row.

These students take one and pass the remainder to the students sitting behind them, much like when we receive a normal handout in class.

Eventually, I get one, too.

It's a blank, completely nondescript piece of recycled paper cut to about four inches on each side.

"Bring them up to me once you've finished writing. That's it."

"Um, what do you mean by 'something'?" Kokone takes it upon herself to ask for the rest of the class.

Otonashi's reply is terse. "My name."

The strange silence from earlier finally breaks as commotion fills the classroom. Which is completely understandable. None of this makes any sense. Her name? Everyone knows that. She just told us this morning when she introduced herself as Aya Otonashi.

"This is stupid," someone spits.

There's only one person who would say something like that to Otonashi: Daiya Oomine.

The entire class seems to gulp in unison. Everyone knows you don't want to get on Daiya's bad side.

"Your name is Aya Otonashi. Sure. What's the point of having everyone write it? Are you desperate to make sure everyone remembers it right away?"

But Otonashi doesn't bat an eye at the harsh remark.

"All I would do is write 'Aya Otonashi.' There, I just showed you I know your name. There's no point in writing it now, right?"

"Fine. I don't care."

Perhaps Daiya wasn't expecting her to agree, because he's at a loss for a retort. With an angry *tch*, he tears his paper up as loudly as possible and leaves the room.

"What's the matter? Hurry up and write."

No one in the classroom has started. Which is completely understandable. Not everyone shows it, but we're completely floored. She just shut Daiya down. As his classmates, we're well aware of how incredible that is.

It's a while before we can do anything. Eventually, the scratch of a mechanical pencil breaks the stillness, and the room gradually fills with sound of other students following suit.

I'm pretty sure no one understands what Otonashi is after, but that doesn't matter.

There's only one thing to write.

Just the name Aya Otonashi.

The first person to bring their paper to Otonashi is Haruaki. Once he's out of his seat, several other students get up as well. There's no substantial change in Otonashi's expression as she takes Haruaki's paper.

I think…*he failed* the test.

"Haruaki." I call him over once he says a couple of words to Mogi and heads back this way.

"What's up, Hosshi?"

"What did you write?"

"Huh? 'Aya Otonashi.' What else would I write? I misspelled it, though." Haruaki looks a bit sad for some reason as he answers.

"…Yeah, I guess that's really the only option."

"C'mon, hurry up and write yours, too."

"But do you think Otonashi is doing this because she actually wants us to write her name?"

If so, then it's hard to believe there's any point to this at all.

"Nope," Haruaki immediately replies.

"Huh? But...you wrote 'Aya Otonashi,' didn't you?"

"I mean... Okay, so Daiyan is ridiculously smart, right? Though, his personality is equally awful."

I cock my head in confusion at the sudden change in topic.

"So Daiya said that all he would write was 'Aya Otonashi.' Which means he couldn't think of anything else to write. I was the same, obviously. We couldn't write something else because we couldn't come up with what that would be."

"So if you can't think of anything...you can't write it."

"Exactly. The point is, none of this is about us."

I get the feeling Haruaki is right on the money. He has to be right.

In other words, Otonashi is ignoring the majority of the class and doing all of this for *someone who could think of something else to write.*

Now I know why Haruaki looked so dejected earlier. I mean, he really does have the hots for Otonashi. His approach was pretty silly, but I've never seen him declare his feelings like that to anyone else, so they must be genuine.

But she isn't falling for it. She won't even give him the time of day... Just like Daiya said.

"...You know, you're smarter than I thought, Haruaki."

"The 'than I thought' part was totally unnecessary."

That actually was pretty rude, so I try to clear the air with a smile. Haruaki is kind enough to return it with a slightly forced grin.

"Anyway, I'll see ya later. My teammates will kill me if I don't get moving. Well, maybe that's an exaggeration, but still."

"Okay. Hang in there."

It must be tough playing for a fairly capable baseball club.

I return to my blank piece of paper. I was figuring I would just write *Aya Otonashi*, but for some reason, I can't bring myself to do it.

I look closely at the girl. There's absolutely no change in her expression as she skims the papers the other students have given her. They all must have the name from her self-introduction on them.

Anyone who can't think of anything else wouldn't be able to write anything else.

"…"

So what am I supposed to do? I mean, I did think of something else. For some reason, the totally random name Maria popped into my head.

No, I get it. My mind is doing something weird. Where the hell did I come up with "Maria," of all things? If I write that and give it to Otonashi, she'll just yell at me to stop messing with her.

But what if, in some wild twist of fate, this happens to be the answer she's hoping for…?

Filled with doubt and uncertainty, I start writing on that four-by-four-inch scrap of recycled paper.

Maria.

I stand up and walk over to Otonashi. There's no line. It seems I'm the last to turn my paper in. Nervously, I hand it to her. She accepts it without a word.

And then she sees what's written on it.

The change in her expression is unmistakable.

"…Huh?"

Neither Mr. Kokubo nor Daiya could get a reaction out of her, so why is she suddenly so wide-eyed?

"Heh-heh-heh…"

And now she's laughing.

"Hoshino."

"Oh, you remembered my name."

I regret that comment instantly. Otonashi's laughter vanishes, and she glares at me like she's finally cornered the man who murdered her parents. "You bastard… Don't mess with me." Her voice is choked, as if it's all she can do to fight down her rage.

I predicted what she would say, but not that tone.

Next thing I know, she has me firmly by the collar of my jacket.

"Whoa! I-I'm sorry! I wasn't trying to…"

"Why else would you write that if you aren't trying to play with me?!"

"Um, well, you see… It's just that, er… Yeah, maybe I was just playing around."

And that probably seals my fate.

Her hands still securely gripping my collar, Otonashi drags me off behind the school.

"Hoshino, do you think you can make fun of me?"

Otonashi has me up against the wall of the school as her eyes bore into me.

"Strategy is not my strong suit. I'm well aware of this. My plans are about as simple and ill-advised as telling the culprit to come out and identify himself. You can't even call them plans. So why the hell are you falling for them?! This is the second time! It's like you're completely ignoring what happened the first time!"

Otonashi has finally released me, but her gaze alone is enough to fix me in place. Seeing my reaction, she presses her lips tight before letting out a sigh.

"...It's just that I felt like I wasn't getting anywhere, so I lost my cool for a bit once I thought I'd made some headway. But the truth is that things are taking a turn for the better, so I suppose I should be happy."

"...Uh, yeah, that's right. You should be happy. Ha-ha-ha."

Otonashi meets my good-natured chuckle with a terrifying glare. I'd probably be better off keeping my mouth shut.

"...I don't understand you. I thought that maybe my persistence had worn you down...but I can't figure out why you look so carefree and empty-headed."

It's not that I'm empty-headed so much as that I have absolutely no clue what she's talking about.

"You ignored me for the first 2,600 times. I could never get you to submit, no matter how many of these endless repetitions I went through. It's exhausting. It should be for you, too, but you always seem perfectly fine."

What should I do? I don't understand a word she's saying.

Perhaps finally realizing how bewildered I am, Otonashi eyes me dubiously.

"......Don't tell me you aren't aware?"

"Aware? Of what?"

"...Have it your way. Whether you're acting or not, I suppose there's no real harm in explaining. Well, to put it simply, I've transferred schools 2,601 times now."

The only response I have to such a claim is to stare in shock.

"If you are acting, you really deserve some kind of award. That's the sort of stupid face you can make only when you're entirely clueless. But whatever. I'll explain things to you as I understand them. Now, then... Today is March second, right?"

I nod.

"It'd be easy if I could just say that I've repeated March second 2,601 times now, but it's not as simple as that. I can't say it's precisely correct, but I use the word 'transfer.'"

"Wha...?"

"I have been returned to 6:27 AM on the morning of March second 2,601 times."

"..."

"'Returned' is the proper expression from my perspective, but it's actually inaccurate. I use the term 'transfer' because it's a bit closer to the truth."

My mouth gapes open, and Otonashi clutches her hair in frustration.

"Agh, I can't take this anymore! Just how stupid are you?! Whenever something inconvenient for you happens after 6:27 AM, you just 'fix' it by making it so it never happened!" she yells, losing her temper.

Hey, come on, now. No one can understand all of that thrown at them out of nowhere, you know.

"I'm not sure I really understand, but are you saying you keep experiencing the same period of time over and over?"

It happens right as those words leave my lips.

"Ah—"

What is this? What's going on?

A massive wave of wrongness washes over me, weighing on my chest. "Wrongness" isn't a strong enough term to describe it, but that's what it is. It's like realizing the town I live in has been switched with an entirely different one, except that everyone else is going about their lives as usual without noticing.

But it's not like lost memories have returned to me. I still don't remember anything, but I can definitely tell that something has happened all the same.

Otonashi is telling me the truth.

"Do you finally understand?"

"H-hold on a minute…"

We've repeated March second 2,601 times. That alone is more than enough to confuse me, but it's the other thing Otonashi is implying that really gets to me…

"And *I'm the one doing this?*"

"Yep," Otonashi answers immediately.

"Wh-why would I do that?"

"I have no way of knowing your motivations."

"But I'm not doing it!"

"You're probably not even aware of it."

Why me? As I ask this, I realize there's only one reason I could have drawn her attention.

I wrote *Maria* on the piece of paper.

"Just as you went through each repetition completely unaware up until now, the other people who are simply caught up in this have had their past erased as well. There was no way for me to make you remember your past that they didn't share. In other words, I've told the name Maria to the entire class, but the only ones who could possibly write it are the culprit and myself."

But I remembered that name. "Maria" had just popped into my head from out of nowhere. That couldn't be normal.

"I don't know if it's been effective or not, but I've done my best to behave in an especially memorable manner. I was waiting for the culprit, who should be the only person besides me with memories of those worlds that never were, to slip up and reveal himself. I didn't have much hope that it would actually work, though."

"…How long have you suspected it was me? I mean, you went to the trouble of telling me the name Maria in one of those past worlds, right?"

"I wouldn't be particularly suspicious of someone as apparently harmless as you."

"So then…"

"Hmph. My time is infinite, so I was just being thorough."

My time is infinite.

I'd like to say it was just a figure of speech, but Otonashi really did spend that much time in her search.

I get it now.

Otonashi has an infinite amount of time, which is what led her to the throwaway strategy of having everyone in the class write her name.

It was all in the slim hope that someone would write *Maria*. No, maybe she wasn't expecting anything at all. Maybe she had run out of ideas during her 2,601 "transfers" and was simply killing time until she could come up with a new plan. In any case, she most likely does have an eternity ahead of her.

That explains why Otonashi is so angry that I fell for her plan. It's like grinding for levels in an RPG to take down that impossible boss, only to find you could have just cheesed him by using a certain item. You achieved your goal all the same, but you wish you could have your wasted time and effort back.

"...No. I lost focus for a moment, but I still can't afford to be careless. Nothing has been resolved, after all."

"Are you sure?"

"Of course I'm sure. Does it look like anything's been solved to you? Does it look like anything about this ongoing nightmare, this 'Rejecting Classroom,' has ended to you?"

Rejecting classroom? She must be referring to the cycle of repetition we're stuck in.

Still, there's one thing that's still bugging me...

"I understand why you're treating me like the one behind all this since I wrote the name Maria, but how is it that you aren't stuck in the Rejecting Classroom like everyone else?"

"It's not that I'm not stuck. I am just as firmly trapped here as the rest of you. If I decide to stop remembering and give up, I'll go through all of this over and over again with no meaning, just like everyone else. It would be as simple as spilling a cup of water balanced on top of my head. We'd repeat for eternity that day you keep rejecting."

"Forgetting is all it would take for that to happen to you?"

"Think about it. Does anyone else seem likely to realize things are repeating themselves? You're the one behind all this, and even you were unaware of what's happening."

...She might be right. We've already gone through all of this 2,601 times, after all.

"It would be effortless for me to stop remembering. But that will absolutely never happen."

"…Never?"

"Never. Giving up is an impossibility for me. I don't care whether we do this two thousand times, two million times, or two billion times—I will triumph and accomplish what I set out to do."

Two thousand times. I give that number some thought. You hear about groups of two thousand relatively often, but when you actually consider adding one plus one plus one all the way up… Well, there are 365 days in a year and 1,825 days in five years, so it's even more than that.

Otonashi has been at this for all that time.

"Hoshino, do you have any idea how you were able to create the Rejecting Classroom?"

"Huh? …No."

"Heh, I see. It would definitely be significant if you were playing dumb to avoid answering. That's some impressive acting, if that's what you're doing."

"Th-this isn't an act."

"Well then, let me just ask you something…"

A faint smile creeps onto Otonashi's face.

"Hoshino, *you've met* _____, *haven't you?*"

Who?

But I can't even ask that obvious question. My mind reels as I try to figure out why. Who have I met? I don't know. I can't remember.

All the same, I understand.

I have indeed met *.

When? Where? Naturally, I don't know either of these things. I have no memory. The one thing I know is *the encounter definitely took place.*

I try to force myself to remember. But for some reason, that information vanishes before I can see it, as if a shutter is slamming down in front of it at incredible speed. *Beep, beep, beep. Access denied. No unauthorized personnel beyond this point.*

"Heh. You did, didn't you?"

Otonashi snickers to herself.

She's certain now. And so am I.

I, Kazuki Hoshino, am the villain responsible for this entire situation.

"You should have received something. A Box that can grant a single wish."

The word "box" is unexpected—but judging by the context, it must be the device that created the Rejecting Classroom.

"That reminds me—I still haven't told you what I'm actually trying to do," says Otonashi, a triumphant smirk still on her face. "My goal is to obtain that Box." And with that, her smile disappears. Now that she's sure I have what she wants, she icily orders, "Now hand it over."

Surely I must have it.

But if this Box really can grant wishes, should I give it to her so easily?

She's put herself through all of this 2,601 times, over and over, just to get this device. She must have a wish she needs to come true, enough to go to such drastic lengths for it. She's so desperate that she would be willing to take the Box and its wish away from me. That's what it boils down to.

That level of persistence definitely isn't normal. It's crazy—beyond a doubt. There's something peculiar about Aya Otonashi.

"I don't know how to give it to you."

It's not a lie. But it's also my sole means of resistance.

"I see. But if you did know, you'd give it to me, right?"

"Well…"

"It's not uncommon to forget. You do know how; you simply can't recall. It's like riding a bicycle—you know what it feels like to do it, but you can't explain it to anyone else. You're just confused because you can't put it into words now."

"…Is there a way to put an end to the Rejecting Classroom without handing over the Box?"

Otonashi's gaze grows even more frigid at my words.

"So you don't want to give it to me after all. Is that what you're trying to say?"

"N-no, that's not it—I just…"

Otonashi quietly sighs as she sees my obvious panic.

"There's a way. If I destroy the body of the 'owner' along with the Box, I'm fairly certain that will spell the end of the Rejecting Classroom."

"Destroy the owner?"

The owner. That probably refers to the culprit who has the Box, which would be me. She has to destroy me? That means…

"If you die, this Rejecting Classroom we're stuck in will end," Otonashi says in a detached voice, as if she's swallowing her emotions.

C'mon. There was no need for the xxxx.

Are you saying this is my future? If so, that despicable act is my only choice. I would almost rather you did this to me now.

It's the morning of March 3. I'm at an intersection with poor visibility due to the rain.

I've cast aside my umbrella, and I'm staring at a xxxx. Nothing else even enters my field of vision. Not even the truck smashed into the fence, or Otonashi standing nearby, draws my gaze from it. A red liquid flows endlessly, the rain powerless to wash it all away.

There's a body with half its head missing and the braixx splattered everywhere. A xxrpse. A cadaver. A stiff. Dead meat. Cold, lifeless flesh. A body. A body! A BODY!

It's Haruaki's.

"—Guagh!"

As I become fully aware of just what is before me, I vomit.

I look at Aya Otonashi. She's watching me, her face expressionless.

"…Haruaki."

Don't worry. Everything's going to be all right, Haruaki.

I mean, we're just going to go back to the beginning of the cycle.

It'll be like none of this ever happened. Lucky for us.

Wait. Did I…?

Did I wish the Rejecting Classroom into existence because I couldn't accept a horrible event like this…?

2,602nd Time

"I'm Aya Otonashi."

*   *   *

"—Guagh!"

In that instant, I'm hit with a flashback to that bloodred scene, locked away in the deepest depths of my memory despite how recently I witnessed it.

That scene is what slowly draws out my memories of the 2,601st transfer, like a thread pulling them directly from my brain.

I'm surprised I could keep myself from screaming.

"Hey, what's the matter, Hosshi? You okay? You look like you're in pain."

Haruaki, *who was sitting in the seat next to me*, expresses his concern.

Even though a truck pulverized him, there he is, smiling and laughing beside me.

The wrongness of it all is overwhelming. I feel nauseated. The information floods over me, devouring me like I'm its prey. My mind can't keep up with the rapid flow and is left completely behind.

My memories of the previous time and my memories of this time have connected.

It's all so sharp and vivid.

"But, man, that Aya is too cute. I'm gonna go profess my love to her."

And it's thanks to Haruaki's lifeless corpse.

Despite meeting such a grisly fate, he's right here, head over heels in love with Aya Otonashi.

I look at the transfer student. At that moment, our eyes meet. She holds my gaze with a bold smirk.

…Was the corpse an attempt to back me into a corner and force me to hand over the Box?

If so, it was tremendously effective. The dead body threatened me with death, and my friend's involvement crushed me with guilt. Otonashi is doing this of her own volition. I understand the rationale that says I'm not responsible, but the sight of that corpse scatters logic to the wind, and my mind simply can't take it.

If I knew how, I would give her the Box right here and now. Fortunately, I have no idea how to do that.

Fortunately? Really? If this is an effective mode of attacking me, Otonashi's going to keep it up.

Until my mind finally breaks for good.

She leaves the podium to stand beside me.

Then, looking straight ahead and not even glancing in my direction, she whispers:

"Looks like you remembered."

At this rate, I'm going to break.

I know all I'm doing is temporarily sidestepping the issue, but I still feign ignorance and avoid Otonashi.

I have to think up a plan while I buy myself some time.

That's why...

"Is that all you wanted to ask me about, Kazu?"

...I'm asking for advice from Daiya Oomine, the smartest person I know.

Daiya doesn't bother to hide his terrible mood as he leans against the wall of the hallway.

It's probably because it took so long to explain everything. The breaks after first and second period, to be exact.

"So now what? You told me *the idea for your little novel*, so what exactly is it you want from me?"

My explanation to Daiya was exhaustive. I hadn't left anything out.

Still, given the nature of the story, I didn't think a down-to-earth realist like Daiya would believe it if I gave it to him straight. Which is why I said it was an idea for a book.

"I was just wondering what the protagonist of this story should do."

"Well, regardless of anything else, he has to fight back against the transfer student."

The protagonist in this situation is, of course, me, while the transfer student is Otonashi.

It was pretty obvious, so Daiya immediately picked up on the real identity of my characters. "Oh, so you based it on her?" he'd said with a smirk. Still, he doesn't really seem to care, since I'm putting it forth as strictly fiction.

"But I don't think the protagonist has any chance of winning."

"You're right. He probably doesn't right now."

My opponent is Aya Otonashi, someone who's gone through 2,602 transfers to get ahold of the Box and isn't afraid of using the corpses of my friends to manipulate me. I can't think of a single item in my arsenal that would allow me to beat her.

"But it's possible that at some point in the future, our hero will get some ability that'll give him a fair chance," Daiya states offhandedly.

"Really?"

Obviously, I came to Daiya in search of a way to oppose Otonashi, but I still feel like I'm grasping at straws. I honestly didn't expect any sort of substantial revelation.

"What's that look for? Fine, let me ask you this: Why doesn't the protagonist have a chance against the transfer student?"

"Huh? Well, that's—"

"No, no, don't answer. A dumbass like you would probably just give me some crap that would piss me off even more."

…Hey, should I be offended?

"So the difference between our hero and the transfer student is really just a difference in the information they have at their disposal. And the transfer student is using that disparity to manipulate the protagonist like a puppet. It's that simple. All he needs is good information that will flip the odds in his favor."

You know…he's right. Otonashi can do whatever she wants with me as long as I keep forgetting everything that's happened.

"Here's another way of putting it: Our protagonist will stand a chance if he can somehow close the gap, since it's the biggest thing keeping him at a disadvantage. He just has to do away with that handicap."

"…But that's not possible," I mutter, and Daiya lets out a snort.

"Hey, you did say the protagonist sometimes keeps his memories from the previous time, right?"

"Yeah."

"If he can carry over the version of him that remembers the previous time, then he can have memories from the previous two times. You see what I'm getting at?"

"……Yeah, that makes sense."

"If he can hold on to memories from the previous two times, then what's to keep him from doing it again and recalling things from three times ago? And if he can do it from three times ago, what's to keep him from doing four times? And so on and so on."

"...That's— I mean, the transfer student will be building up information the whole time, too. He'll never catch up and fill the gap. Otona—I mean, the transfer student already has over 2,601 loops' worth of information under her belt. Just two or three isn't going to be enough for the hero to—"

"Then do it 100,000 times."

"...What?"

"Sure, he's never going to make up for those 2,601 times that are already said and done, so he should just render them meaningless instead. Once it's been 102,601 times, though, the simple math says that gap of 2,601 will only equate to a measly two percent of his 100,000 transfers. I'd hardly call that a disparity. With that many repetitions, our hero will have what he needs to take her on. With the knowledge he's gained and the effort he makes her expend, he can wear down the transfer student until she's weak enough that she forgets about the cycle of repetition."

"Really?"

Can I really do that?

"...But what if he doesn't know how to carry over his memories?"

It's true. I held on to my memories this time, but that was just a coincidence.

"You said the hero was able to keep his memories because the shock of seeing the dead body overwhelmed him, right?"

"Yeah...I think that's why it happened."

It's the only reason I can come up with, at least, and my intuition tells me I'm right.

Seeing Haruaki's lifeless body somehow allowed me to hold on to my memories for once.

"Then it's simple," Daiya says flippantly. *"Our little protagonist needs to start making some corpses of his own."*

"—What?!"

I'm speechless.

"B-but I can't—"

"Just listen. It's definitely too much to have him actually kill somebody. A protagonist without any morals like that would just make your readers mad. That's not what I'm talking about here. What I'm saying is that the hero needs to devise his own situations to shock himself, something on the level of seeing a dead body."

"...Well, yeah, that would definitely work..."

"What it all boils down to at this point is that the protagonist needs be even more persistent about the Box than his rival."

The bell rings, and Daiya turns his back on me, signaling that my audience with him is at an end.

"I'm going back to the classroom. You should hurry, too."

"Okay..."

I don't feel like going straight to class, though, so I stay where I am a bit longer. Daiya walks off without me.

I sigh.

"...Maybe there is a way to get through this without forgetting. But still..."

...I'd need to make it through one hundred thousand transfers. It's logically possible, of course, but it isn't feasible. There's no way a human being could withstand the actual experience. It's like asking me to take a ride in a car that could go ten thousand miles per hour just because it exists. The car might be able to go that fast, but the pressure would crush me. My—no, *any* normal human being's mind would crack under the strain of one hundred thousand cycles.

If Otonashi can do it, then there's something special about her. I never want to be the same as a monster like her.

But what if that really is the only way to beat her? Should I even be in this fight in the first place? Maybe it would be better for both of us if I just meekly raise the white flag of surrender.

I can't even decide on that now, and I let out another long sigh.

Just when I raise my head and get moving back to the classroom...

"Ah!"

I can't stop myself from calling out.

"...Haruaki."

Did he hear us? Even if he didn't, the look on his face as he emerges from behind the pillar is too grave.

All we were doing was talking about a novel, a work of fiction. For the most part.

"You know how jealous I get when I hear my friends hanging out without me. I'm A-OK with hiding and eavesdropping when I get that way. You'll cut me some slack, right?"

Haruaki begins defending his actions without even being asked to. He talks as if he's just joking around, but his expression stays serious the whole time.

"Now then, Hosshi..."

Haruaki scratches his head as he continues.

"...You want to try killing me?"

My breath catches in my throat.

Why on earth would he say that? It's completely unlike him.

Haruaki watches me for a moment as I stand there in shock. I can't even blink. After a moment, a satisfied smile rises on his face before he bursts into laughter as if he can't hold it in any longer.

"I knew it! That was horrible, Haruaki! Don't mess with me like that!"

"Ah-ha-ha-ha! I never thought you'd get so serious! Wow! You're hilarious, Hosshi! Of course I was kidding!"

Yeah, he's right. I don't think anyone in their right mind would believe that the cycle of repetition we just talked about is actually occurring.

"Yeah, I know... You were just joking, weren't you?"

"Of course I was. How could that be anything else? As if I would let you kill me!"

Something feels off about that last part.

"...Haruaki?"

"Yeah? What do you need my help with?"

Help? What is he talking about?

Haruaki is dead serious again.

"Well, I guess there's only so much I can do since I'm going to lose my memories the next time the world starts over, but all the same, I'd like to lend you a hand."

Ah, now I get it.

Haruaki believes in the Rejecting Classroom.

The whole thing sounds absolutely ridiculous, but he believes it.

"...Haruaki."

"What's the matter, Hosshi?"

"Um... All of that was just a scenario I thought up."

Haruaki laughs loudly at that and remarks matter-of-factly, "C'mon, you're lying, right?"

"Wh...?"

What? The word sticks in my throat before I can even ask.

If someone asked me to believe all this nonsense, I know I certainly wouldn't.

"Wah-ha-ha-ha! What, are you moved by the depths of our friendship because I swallowed that story of yours, no questions asked?"

"Yeah."

When I nod, Haruaki suddenly looks a bit taken aback.

"C'mon now... Don't be so serious. You'll make me blush."

He turns a bit red and scratches his nose.

"Let me tell you something. Even Daiyan knows everything you described is really happening to you and not just some crazy story you cooked up."

"Huh? ...No, there's no way. He's a realist."

Now that he mentions it, though, Daiya seemed a little unlike his usual self earlier.

After all, he did meet me where I asked him to come, and he spent his entire break time hearing me out. If he really thought this was all some idea for a novel, he would've called it a bunch of crap and left right then and there.

"I doubt he's taking everything you're saying at face value, but I get the feeling he truly believes you're stuck in the situation you described."

Daiya's ideas certainly were a little peculiar for writing advice. The answers he provided were precisely what I was looking for.

"It doesn't add up, Hosshi. You based the transfer student on Aya, right? But she only transferred to our class today. You asked Daiya for advice during our first period break. When did you have the time to put that whole story together?"

"Ah—"

He's exactly right.

"For me, at least, I think your story is true and not some crazy delusion."

"...Why?"

"You have to admit this is way better than the other crap you usually come up with. Your imagination just isn't that good."

"Hey, that's mean..."

"But I would have believed it even if you were really smart, or at least the type who could whip up a story like that off the top of his head."

"...Why?"

"'Cause you're my friend."

Whoa, what's this guy saying?

Now I'm blushing. C'mon, how am I supposed to respond to that?

Haruaki's eyebrows furrow as he pops a fry into his mouth.

"I see. So it's looking like our sweet Aya...well, Aya Otonashi is the one who killed me."

We're at McDonald's at Haruaki's suggestion. It's the middle of the afternoon, and we're sitting in the restaurant still in our school uniforms, having left early for the day after falsely claiming to be ill. I keep fidgeting, worried about the gazes of others around us.

"I wonder if she could sit in McDonald's in her uniform at this time of day without feeling weird."

"I'm sure Aya Otonashi could pull it off."

Though Haruaki has supposedly fallen for her, there's definitely animosity in his voice as he says her full name.

"That's probably because she's used to it after going through all this more than two thousand times."

Otonashi is used to things going back to as if they had never happened. She isn't going to get worked up about the events of the Rejecting Classroom anymore.

Which means she's adjusted to all this craziness. Can she even really be considered sane anymore?

She *is* potentially trying to kill me.

"I suppose you think you've escaped from me."

My heart freezes in my chest.

The voice of the person I was just thinking of came from nowhere. I can't turn around, even though I heard its source behind me. I'm as mobile as concrete.

Why is she here? We didn't even tell Daiya where we were going.

Otonashi circles around in front of us. I can't lift my gaze to look at her.

"I'll let you in on something, Hoshino," she says with a smirk. "I've experienced March second 2,602 times now. I've spent all that time with my classmates who are completely unaware they're repeating the same day over and over. They haven't changed in the slightest."

She quietly places her white hands on the table. Just that is enough to petrify me.

"People change. Their values change. It's no simple matter to predict their behavior. However, it's pathetically easy to predict the actions of scum trapped in a stagnant puddle like you. Especially when it's March second every time. I know all your conversation patterns. Predicting the behavior of a fairly inactive high school student like you couldn't be easier, Hoshino."

I'm all too aware of the information advantage Daiya described. Before, my understanding was that he was referring to details about the Rejecting Classroom or the Box, but that wasn't necessarily the case. The most problematic knowledge she has at her disposal is what she has on me, Kazuki Hoshino. By the same token, what I need to get my hands on is info about Aya Otonashi. That's what Daiya was trying to tell me from the get-go and why he told me that going through the repetitions would allow me to whittle away at the gap between us.

"Do you understand now? There is no escape for you, Hoshino. You're firmly in my grasp. It would be so easy to crush you if I wanted to, but if I did, I would also lose the valuable object in your possession. That's the only reason I'm holding back. So I hope you understand. You'd better not do anything to make me angry."

Otonashi grabs my hand.

"Stay quiet and come with me. Do what I say and keep your mouth shut."

Her grip isn't strong. I could shake it off easily if I wanted to, but am I capable of that...? No, I'm not. Aya Otonashi has absorbed me completely. I know it sounds pathetic. All the same, I just can't oppose her. I don't even know how.

Still, despite my utter inability to fight back, Otonashi lets go of me.

"What do you think you're doing?" she says.

I haven't shaken off her hand, so her hostile question isn't directed at me.

"What're you doing?! ...Ah!"

It's for Haruaki, who pulled Otonashi's hand off me.

"I'm not going to let you take Hosshi. Don't you get that? Are you stupid or something?"

Haruaki's challenge sounds childish, and his face is tense. He's definitely acting. I've never known Haruaki to censure others like this.

Naturally, his obvious bluff isn't enough to move Otonashi.

"That's not what I'm asking. You're the one with dull wits, Usui. Your actions are futile. Meaningless. It seems you've decided to help Hoshino, but all of that is part of a waking dream that will shortly fade to nothingness. Next time, you won't see me as an enemy. You'll probably even profess your love to me again."

Haruaki recoils under the verbal assault, probably because he knows it's all true. Once the world is reset, he'll forget everything he discussed with me today. She's his enemy now, but when the next loop comes around, he'll be just as infatuated with her as before. He's stuck in a mire of despair.

Despite having been confronted with this truth, Haruaki is still clenching his fists.

"No, I still think you're the one having trouble understanding, Otonashi. Sure, I might get reset each time so that I have no clue what's going on. I can't hold on to my memories, and I'm not smart like Daiya. But I know I can trust myself."

"I don't understand. What are you getting at?"

"Think about it, Otonashi. Are you positive I'm completely incapable of change?"

"Of course. You can't do anything."

"Ha! You've got it backward. If I can't change, that also means I can guarantee certain things will be true for me in the next reality. After all, I'm going to be exactly the same person I was this time. It's easy to imagine. As long as Hosshi explains things to me, I know I'll trust him and lend him a hand every step of the way. I'd never abandon a friend like Hosshi, no matter what reality we're in. You keep that in mind, Otonashi."

Haruaki jabs a finger at her as he continues.

"As long as Kazuki Hoshino is your enemy, then you've made an enemy of me as well. And I can never die."

To be honest, his pose as he makes his declaration isn't remotely impressive. It's forced, he's obviously trying to put up a strong front, and his hands are shaking. There's no hiding how frightened he is. Haruaki's usually a complete goofball. He'll never be able to deliver cool lines like that convincingly.

Still, it's more than enough to warm my heart.

He may look silly, but there isn't a single hint of doubt in his voice. No fancy words. He's just saying what comes naturally to him.

"…"

Otonashi is, of course, unfazed by Haruaki and his slightly awkward stance.

But she doesn't have an immediate comeback for him, either. Her lips purse together in an unpleasant grimace for several seconds.

"You speak like you think I'm the evil one here, even though it's because of Kazuki Hoshino that we're trapped in the Rejecting Classroom."

Otonashi's words are pointed and precise. I can see them hitting home with Haruaki. But still…

"I don't make mistakes when it comes to choosing friends."

Haruaki's opinion will not be swayed. He's frightened, but he refuses to look away.

I'm getting worried. This is Aya Otonashi we're dealing with. She isn't the one who's going to suffer from having a permanent enemy. Haruaki is. Each time, someone he's naturally attracted to is going to treat him with resentment for what appears to be no reason. He's setting himself up for an endless cycle of pain.

All the while, Otonashi is never going to feel an iota of pressure, no matter how much Haruaki snaps at her.

Still…

"This is getting tedious."

Otonashi is the first to avert her gaze and turn away.

"All your actions here today will just be rendered meaningless, anyway."

And with that, she leaves.

If it were anyone besides Otonashi, I might've called them a sore loser.

But it didn't sound that way at all. She didn't seem to have taken anything Haruaki said to heart, so I wonder when she decided it was okay to accept defeat this time.

I guess that's why she said exactly what she thought. She concluded it would be easier to manage us when the circumstances were more agreeable.

Otonashi doesn't harbor any emotion whatsoever toward us. She isn't afraid of us, naturally, but she also doesn't bear any anger or contempt toward us.

So…why did she…?

No, I know the reason—it was just my imagination. I was mistaken. I clearly read the situation incorrectly. Still, it really, really seemed, just for a second, that I saw a touch of sadness pass across her face.

"Hey, Hosshi!"

Haruaki speaks, still eying the automatic door Otonashi left through moments earlier.

"Do you think I'm gonna get killed?"

My first instinct is to say there's no way that could happen, but when I realize he might be right, I swallow the words.

In the end, it's raining on the morning of the 2,602nd March 3. Even though I take a longer route to avoid the scene of the accident, I end up arriving at school early.

It isn't so much that I want to avoid Otonashi's attack as I just never want to witness anything like that ever again.

Daiya is already in the classroom when I arrive. He approaches as soon as he catches sight of me.

"What's up, Daiya?"

Something keeps him from answering right away. He's peering closely at my eyes. While he's still as skilled as ever at keeping his thoughts hidden, there's clearly something unusual going on.

"...So, hey, about that book idea we were talking about yesterday..."

Daiya's tone is intentionally light as he mentions my novel, or more precisely, my beliefs about how things are occurring.

"I was curious about something. Why doesn't the transfer student lose her memories each time like the protagonist does?"

I don't have a good response, probably because I don't know why he's bringing this up.

"The protagonist can't hold on to his memories even though he's the one responsible for creating the Rejecting Classroom. Even if the transfer student has some special ability, doesn't it seem a little cheap for her to automatically keep her memories after each repetition? I think you should make it so both characters have to use the same methods to maintain their memories."

"...You might be right."

I agree without thinking about the implications too much. I'm not entirely sure what he's trying to say, I guess because Daiya's still talking like this is all for a novel.

"The hero's able to retain his memories because he sees a dead body, right?"

"...I think so."

"And he sees the body because someone got hit by a truck, correct? There's no way the transfer student, who has experienced this same day 2,601 times, didn't know that truck was going to lose control. So if she's somehow involved in this accident, you can be sure she meant for it to happen. That's why you presented the death of the hero's friend as a murder."

I nod.

"But that's what bothers me."

"What? Is there something wrong with that approach?"

"No, you're on the right track. It was most definitely an attack on the protagonist. What I'm getting at is that maybe witnessing the accident was a prerequisite for him to keep his memories. There's no point to the attack if he's just going to forget it all right away."

"I'm not sure what you're trying to tell me here…"

"So the transfer student wants to take the Box from the protagonist, right?"

"Right."

"Try thinking from her perspective. She's finally found her guy, the one she's been searching for. She could've just kept quiet, but instead she goes to the trouble of explaining everything to him. Which opponent would it be easier to take the Box from—one who's completely oblivious, or one who's on guard? The oblivious one, of course. If that's the case, then why do you think she bothers explaining everything to him?"

"Ummm… I guess because she thinks he's going to forget?"

"That's right. She judges there isn't any harm in telling him. Explaining everything to the protagonist is probably a bit of a pastime for her at this point. You could even call it careless."

"But she had to have set up the accident, right? Which means it could only have been an attack on me, so…?"

"I'm sure she set it up. But try thinking of it this way: The transfer student didn't expect the protagonist to see the body."

So in other words, she caused the accident for some other purpose than attacking me?

I think over our conversation again.

"Ah—"

I hurriedly look around the classroom. The transfer student, Aya Otonashi, is nowhere to be found. She's probably still at the scene of the accident.

"It can't be… She's insane!"

"Of course she is. There's no way someone who's adjusted to living the same day 2,602 times could be right in the head."

Aya Otonashi is killing people.

Not as an attack on me, *but as a way of retaining her memories.*

I remembered. I didn't want to, but I remembered. The 2,601st time wasn't the first time that accident took place. It could have happened 2,600 times before then.

If this is true, does it mean that Otonashi kills someone each time she transfers?

Can I really just sit back and let this happen?

Is Haruaki going to be murdered this time, too?

"Haruaki!"

"Huh? What's up, Hosshi?"

Standing over by the door is the man himself, who's just arrived.

What does this mean? If he isn't the victim, then... Oh. The dead body doesn't necessarily have to be Haruaki's, it seems.

"That's enough about your book for now, Kazu. Let's get down to the real matter at hand." Daiya continues on, paying no mind to Haruaki. "I heard there was an accident just now."

He pauses a breath, then speaks.

"A truck hit Aya Otonashi."

Um, what the—?

Oh, I get it.

It works perfectly fine if she's the victim, too.

4,609th Time

"A truck hit Haruaki."

5,232nd Time

"A truck hit Kasumi Mogi."

27,753rd Time

It's soccer day in PE.

I have a bloody nose, and I'm resting my head on Mogi's lap. She's still in her regular school uniform.

I suddenly wonder what prompted Mogi to say I could rest my head on her. Is this the kind of thing she would do if she was trying to win me over?

I glance up at her face, but all I can see is the same vacant expression she always has, as if there's nothing on her mind at all.

"...Hey, Mogi?"

"What is it?"

"What're you thinking about?"

"Huh?"

Mogi tilts her head, but no answer is forthcoming. Her only response is a puzzled look.

I mull this over. Would it be impossible to build a romantic relationship with such a blank slate?

Why do I have feelings for a girl as confusing as Mogi?

And when exactly did they start?

I try to remember.

"......Huh?"

"...What is it?" asks Mogi at my sudden outburst.

"Oh, uh... It's nothing."

I'm sure my expression exposes my lie. Mogi can see that, but she isn't prepared to pry further, so she just closes her mouth.

I get up without protest from her.

"Well... It looks like the bleeding stopped."

"...Yeah."

That's the extent of our conversation.

Why did I voluntarily end what would normally be an awesome situation? I might never be that happy again ever in my life.

But I just can't.

I mean, I can't *remember*.

I can't remember. I can't remember. I can't remember! *I can't remember when I started to like Mogi!*

Why am I attracted to her? What about her caught my eye? Did I just find myself drawn to her for no real reason?

I should know at least that—there's no reason I shouldn't, but for the life of me I can't recall any of it.

It wasn't love at first sight. I've never interacted with Mogi outside of school.

So when did it all happen? Did my love just bloom out of nothing?

"—It can't be."

There's no way it could be true, but it's the only thing I can imagine. *My love for Mogi just appeared out of thin air.*

"What's wrong? Are you okay? ...Maybe you need to go to the nurse's office," says Mogi in a wispy voice.

But even so, I'm over the moon that she's worried about me. I'm happy, pure and simple. There's no way this feeling could be anything but real.

"...I'm fine. I was just thinking about something."

I ask myself over and over if I'm wrong, but the more I do, the more convinced I am it's true:

I wasn't interested in Mogi.

And when did that change? That's right...

...It was yesterday.

"Oh, I see."

I look over at the transfer student, Aya Otonashi, where she stands stock-still in the middle of the schoolyard.

When did my feelings for Mogi blossom? The answer is simple. It wasn't yesterday, even though I'm definitely head over heels for her today. So when, exactly?

It would be impossible during the short time between yesterday and today.

So it could have happened only during the more than twenty thousand times the Rejecting Classroom put me through all this.

There it is. I remember now. It's just a fragment, but it's probably the most I've been able to recall up to this point. Still, it's the barest sliver of a recollection, and any substantial memory remains as lost as all the others to me.

The memory of how I fell in love with Mogi, a memory I should cherish above all others, slipped away from me. I'm sure I'll continue to lose it each time. I can't share anything with her. Nothing can change that, no matter how many times we go through this. My one-sided love will only grow, never to be acted upon.

Maybe that's not what I should be concerned about, though. It's possible the end of the Rejecting Classroom could also spell the end of my romantic feelings for Mogi. After all, they would never have existed without the classroom, right?

It feels wrong. That can't possibly be right. There's absolutely no way these feelings could be a lie.

But if they were never actually possible in the first place, what are they if not false?

A sudden gust of wind blows before the end of class. It lifts Mogi's skirt. I'm not sure why, but in some corner of my mind I get the sense I already knew she'd be wearing light-blue underwear.

Yeah, I definitely did.

I knew the color of her underwear today. And I know that Kasumi Mogi is the one Aya Otonashi sacrifices most frequently in order to retain her memories.

That's what settles it for me.

I'll make sure this Rejecting Classroom never ends.

Aya Otonashi doesn't initiate any contact with me on this loop.

This isn't a first, though. I get the feeling she didn't last time, either.

My memories are hazy, but it seems she hasn't been trying to mess with me at all recently.

It's our lunch break, and Aya Otonashi is sitting apart from the others in the classroom, nibbling a piece of bread as if it's just a tasteless form of sustenance.

I approach her.

Just being near Otonashi is enough to make my body tense and my heart rate skyrocket. Her rejection of others seems vastly greater than before, as if it's physically pushing me away.

"…Otonashi."

Speaking to her takes considerable willpower, but she doesn't turn to look at me. At this distance, there's no way she didn't hear. That's why I continue anyway.

"We need to talk about something."

"Not with me, you don't."

Shut down just like that.

"Otonashi."

No response. She keeps munching her bread with distaste.

I guess she intends to ignore me no matter what I say. If I want a response, I'll have to do something she can't tune out.

After a bit of thought, the perfect thing pops into my head.

"...Maria."

The listless chewing suddenly ceases.

"We need to talk about something."

Not even that is enough to get her to spare me a glance, but she nods without a word.

Stillness has overtaken the classroom. Everyone's holding their breath, waiting to see what happens next.

Perhaps realizing she's lost this little battle of wills, Otonashi eventually sighs in exhaustion.

"You must be remembering quite a bit this time if you can say that name."

"Yeah, that's why I—"

"But there's still nothing for us to talk about."

And with that, Otonashi goes back to apathetically eating her bread.

"Why?!"

The attention of the room turns toward me at my unexpected outburst.

"What's your problem? I'm the one you're supposed to be doing something about, right? How come you won't listen to what I have to say?!"

"Why?" Otonashi snorts in derision. "You seriously don't get it, do you? Ha! Guess I shouldn't be surprised. You're always a complete idiot like this. You couldn't figure anything out by yourself if you tried. Why did I have to end up stuck with you?"

"...I don't know what some other me did in another time, but—"

"Some other you? Don't be stupid. Why do you think another you would be any different from this you? You're exactly the same."

"What makes you so sure? I could say that I want to help you. If I did, then—"

"That wouldn't matter in the slightest." Otonashi cuts me off vehemently, not even waiting to hear the rest of the sentence.

My plan was to match her word for word, but her onslaught is enough to overwhelm any comeback.

"*It's because this isn't the second or even the third time you've said these exact words to me.*"

"Huh?"

There must be something amusing about my dumbstruck expression, because Otonashi smirks slightly and puts her half-eaten bread back in its bag.

"Fine. What's a little more worthless time spent? I've already explained this to you more than a few times, too, so I might as well do it again."

Otonashi stands up and walks off.

All I can do is shut up and follow her.

Otonashi leads me to the usual spot behind the school. As always, she leans against the wall of the building.

"Let's get one thing straight: This is not a discussion. All you're going to do is clean out your ears like a good little fool and listen."

"…I'll do whatever I want."

With a cold glare, Otonashi effortlessly brushes aside my feeble attempt at resistance. "Do you know how many times it's been now, Hoshino? I'm sure you don't. This is the 27,753rd time."

What an absurd number.

"…Are you really keeping count of them all?"

"Yes, because if I stop counting even once, there's no way to go back and check how many times it's been. If I lose track of that, then I'll lose all sense of where I am. That's why I keep count."

That makes sense. If you have no idea where you started, at least knowing how many steps you've taken would bring a tiny bit of relief.

"That's how many times we've been through this all. I've exhausted every approach with you. I can't come up with anything else to try."

"That's why you think it's pointless to talk to me."

"Yeah."

"And you've tried persuading me to give you the Box?"

"I gave up on that a long time ago."

"Why? I'm sure out of all those loops, there must've been at least one when I was easy to win over."

"Yeah, of course there was. There were times when you were hostile and times when you were cooperative. But the thing is, none of that matters. Regardless of your attitude, you haven't given up the Box even once."

Even my cooperative self hasn't handed it over... That seems clear when I think about it. If Otonashi ever did get ahold of the Box, our current reality inside the Rejecting Classroom would no longer exist.

"And you're absolutely sure that I have it?"

"I've always harbored some doubts, but the conclusion I reach is the same every time. There is no doubt that you, Kazuki Hoshino, are the owner of the Box."

"Why is that?"

"There aren't as many possible suspects as you seem to believe. Explaining the ins and outs of why that is would take forever, so I'll make it short. Suffice to say, it would be impossible for this small range of suspects to maintain their deception for all 27,753 times. That's why you are the only conceivable owner of the Box. Besides, you have some irrefutable proof, yourself, right?"

She's correct. I have met *, the Box's distributor.

"Even so, you never bring it out. Rather, you can't. You've never been able to in any of the twenty-thousand-plus times that have passed since I identified you as the owner."

"That's why you've given up?"

Someone like Otonashi, who would do anything to get the Box, has thrown in the towel?

"No, I haven't. There's simply no means of getting it from you. It's like when you're convinced there's a hundred-yen coin in your wallet, but you can't find it no matter how much you dig. Of course, the first thing you do is search every last bit of space inside the wallet. But even then, it doesn't turn up. The only thing you can do at that point is reason that maybe the coin isn't in there after all. Over the course of these 27,753 times, I have concluded that, just like the coin in the wallet, it is absolutely impossible to get the Box out of Kazuki Hoshino."

After one final scowl, Otonashi turns away from me.

"Anyway, that's the end of this farce. Is there anything else you'd like to say?"

"...There is. That's why I wanted to talk to you in the first place."

I have to say it.

I've made up my mind. I'm going to protect the Rejecting Classroom. If Otonashi is going to murder Mogi over and over, then I...

"Otonashi—Aya Otonashi, you..."

"'...Are my enemy from now on,' right?"

"Wha—?!"

Otonashi beats me to the punch, finishing the desperate declaration that was taking so much effort for me to say.

She isn't even looking at me, as if she couldn't care less.

After a weary sigh, utterly disgusted at my speechless astonishment, she turns back toward me as if she has no other choice.

"You still don't get it, do you, Hoshino? How long do you think I've had to put up with you and your idiocy? This is just another routine we've gone through so many times it makes me sick. There's no way I wouldn't know what you planned to say."

"B-but—"

Was I always this determined each time? Was my resolve always meaningless?

"I'll share something else with you. Even when you get up the nerve to make me your enemy, even when you try with all your might to carry over your memories, you never seem to care in the end."

"B-but that's...!"

That would mean I'm allowing Mogi to be murdered. That would mean I'm choosing to lose my feelings for her.

"Don't believe me? Should I tell you the reason you yourself have given me dozens of times?"

I clench my jaw.

Otonashi turns her back on me, signaling that this conversation is at an end.

"That conviction of yours has never wavered even after more than twenty thousand times, I'll give you that."

I rise without thinking.

Did Otonashi just imply that she respects me?

"Wait." There's one thing I haven't asked her yet.

She looks back at me over her shoulder.

I continue. "You aren't trying to take the Box from me anymore?"

"That's what I said, yes."

"Then what are you going to do now?"

Nothing changes in her expression. She simply stares at me, her gaze steady and unwavering.

I can't help it; confronted by such brazen eyes, I'm the first to look away.

"Ah…"

Otonashi suddenly marches off without another word, much less an answer to my question.

Otonashi must've gone straight home, because she's not in the classroom when I return.

It's fifth period. I still can't make heads or tails of these math equations I must have heard thousands of times now, so I give up on paying attention and concentrate on Mogi instead.

Could I really abandon her to her fate? Could my feelings for her dissolve just like that?

No. It's impossible. I don't care what reasons those past versions of me may have had.

All that matters is that the current me can't give up on her.

Fifth period ends.

I make a beeline for Mogi. Noticing my approach, she gazes back at me with her big eyes. That alone is enough to make my body go as rigid as stone. My heart skips a beat or two.

That's what power she has over me. That's how much what I'm about to do means to me.

I'm planning to do something that I would never, ever consider doing under normal circumstances.

I have no other choice, though. It's the only way I can think of to hold on to my memories.

My only option is to tell Mogi how I feel.

"Mogi…"

I'm sure I look nuts, what with my nervousness and the other thoughts racing through my mind. Mogi tilts her head and gives me a curious look.

"Hey, I need to tell you something…"

"Wait until tomorrow."

"Ah…"

Something like a scene from a movie forms in my head, the audio playing whether I want it to or not. The image is clear, bright, and painful, like having my eyes, eardrums, and brains smashed through a pane of glass.

My heart starts pounding, like a hammer slamming into my ribcage.

N-no!

I don't want to remember. I don't want to remember any of this! I tried so hard to erase it, but it never went away. So many other important things flee my mind each time, but this one memory always remains.

Yeah. I'm sure of it.

I've confessed to her before.

"…Are you all right?"

"……Sorry, forget I said anything."

I walk away from Mogi. She frowns as if she doesn't believe me, but she doesn't pursue the matter any further.

I return to my seat and slump over the desk.

"……I get it now."

It's all so obvious once I think about it. It's not like this hasn't played out over twenty thousand times now.

I profess my love to Mogi, but then I forget. So I profess my love again, and I forget again. I've made this confession that I never even wanted to make over and over and over again, all to resist the effects of the Rejecting Classroom, only to forget I had even done so.

And each time, I get the last response in the world I want to hear. It's always the same. The only reply I ever get is the absolute worst one. It's set in stone. There's no reason to think Mogi's answer will ever change if she can't retain her memories.

That answer is—

"Wait until tomorrow."

It's the worst possible thing she could say, *because for us there will never be a tomorrow.*

With the most determination I've ever had in my life, I muster up courage I never knew I had, my nerves frayed to the breaking point, only to have my words vanish into nothingness as if they were never spoken. To make it worse, I'm forced to initiate this interaction even though she's forgotten my profession of love so many times before.

…But I see the truth now. There's no way to erase the past.

There was never anything there to begin with.

This world has been hollow from the very beginning. Nothing, absolutely nothing, holds any value in a world that's about to vanish from existence. Beautiful, disgusting, noble, crude, lovable, hateful—none of it is worth jack here.

That's why there's nothing in this place. It's empty.

This irredeemable void is the Rejecting Classroom.

I feel like throwing up. I'm standing here breathing, but I want to rid my body of that air and everything else. If I do that, I won't be here anymore, though. I can't live without air, but if I inhale the emptiness of this world, I'll become empty, too. I'll suck up all the emptiness like some sort of sponge.

Or maybe all this fretting is too late, and I'm already empty.

"What's the matter, Kazu? Are you sick?"

From my slumped-over position, I slowly lift my head at the familiar voice.

Kokone is standing there with obvious concern.

"You got a bloody nose during PE, right? Maybe that's what it is. If you're not feeling well, maybe I should walk you to the nurse's office."

"Don't worry about him, Kiri. It's not the nosebleed that's messing with him—it's the lap pillow he got afterward."

This comes from Daiya, who's now suddenly nearby.

"A lap pillow…? Ohhh, I get it now! That's got to be it! Aw, is somebody feeling a little lovesick?"

Kokone pounds me on the shoulder, a huge grin on her face.

"Well, well! I never thought you'd be so forward, Kazu! Don't go thinking you're Don Juan now!"

"I have to admit, I'm kinda surprised such a cheap seduction tactic had that effect on you."

"N-no, that's not it! I've always—"

I catch myself midsentence.

I was about to make a serious slip of the tongue, in more ways than one. I would have admitted I had feelings for Mogi, and even more important...

"Huh? I could've sworn you didn't think Mogi was anything special before yesterday."

...it wouldn't have been true.

Today is when I started liking her. I guess at least to Daiya and the others it probably seems like something that came out of the blue. Oh, I get it... That's why none of them noticed my love for Mogi despite it being so plain to see.

"C'mon, Daiya. The real news is that the boy has finally admitted he has a crush on Kasumi, hee-hee!"

Kokone gives Daiya a little jab with her elbow as she giggles.

"True. This could keep me entertained for a while."

"Heh-heh, meddling in other people's romance is so much fun! Now, don't you worry there, Kazu. Your big sis here is in your corner! I'll provide all the advice and assistance you could ever want! I'll even help cheer you up if she blows you off. But it'll be annoying if things actually work out between you, so if that happens, I'll just kill you."

"Don't worry. If they end up going out, I'll steal her away from him."

"Oooh, fun! Nothing beats a little misery and a sordid love triangle!"

...Those two are really the lowest of the low, kicking me while I'm down like this.

But I'm glad at least Xxxxxxx isn't here. If he were around, this whole situation would really run out of control once he was on board.

"...Huh?"

"Aw, what is it, Kazu?"

"No, it's just that I was wondering where that jerk is. Maybe home sick?"

"Who's 'that jerk'?" asks Daiya with a puzzled look.

That's funny. I thought Daiya would know who I'm talking about instantly just by my tone.

"What do you mean 'who'? The only jerk I'd be talking about is..."

...Um, who?

Whoa, hold on a second. I was just about to say someone's name, but now I can't even remember it, much less his or her face.

"...Uh, Kazu? Hello? Who were you talking about?"

I feel ill, with an urge to scrape out my esophagus, as if some thick, viscous slime is stuck in my throat. But it's a good thing that I feel this way. If I can choke it all down and purge it from my body, then Xxxxxxx will be gone.

"H-hey...Kazu!"

I remember now; it's okay. I can remember precisely because I feel sick like this.

"...Haruaki."

That's the name of my best friend, the one who swore he would stand with me forever.

I have just the faintest glimmer of hope. It's possible that I'm the only one who's forgotten Haruaki through some random slip in my memory. But by now I should know how foolish of me it is to even hope for that...

"Hey, Kazu, who's Haruaki?" Daiya asks, but it's a meaningless question.

I grit my teeth in frustration. Daiya and Kokone are curiously watching my behavior.

Both of them have no recollection of Haruaki, even though he's their childhood friend, and they've both known him for much longer than I have.

The truth that Haruaki no longer exists here brutally pierces my heart.

"I'm going home."

The resulting wound is fatal.

I stand up, grab my bag, turn away from Daiya and Kokone, and leave the classroom.

I can't stand to be there for even a second longer.

Why is Haruaki gone?

I know the answer. I know it all too well. Haruaki was *rejected*.

By who? I know that, too. The only one who could have rejected Haruaki is the "protagonist" of this little story, the one who brought the Rejecting Classroom into existence.

I was mistaken to think this endless loop was meant to preserve the normalcy of my daily life forever. How stupid. That was never it at all. The mundane is only normal because it continues to flow onward. If you dam a river, it fills with mud and silt until it becomes pitch-black. That's exactly what this is—a growing reservoir of foul, stagnant water and scum.

Yeah, I see it now. I'm sure I must have stumbled upon this truth many times before. Time and time again, I arrived at this same realization. That's why I decided to stop viewing Aya Otonashi as an enemy.

Aya Otonashi is trying to destroy the Rejecting Classroom.

Why would I stop her?

The bell rings. I'm sure all my classmates must be here by now. I turn back to scan the room before I leave.

An empty seat. Another one. And another. Another over there. Yeah… I knew some desks would be empty, but it still seems strange that no one is questioning why there are so many.

The truth is that I knew all along. I just didn't want to admit it, so I blocked that knowledge from my mind.

Aya Otonashi has figured out that it's impossible to take the Box from me.

Still, putting an end to the Rejecting Classroom would be a simple matter once the one responsible for its creation was identified. Aya went through twenty thousand repetitions even after figuring out I was the culprit, just so she could get the Box.

So what am I going to do now?

I don't even need to think about it.

The truck sends my limbs flying upon impact. The sight of the right leg I've known all my life lying so far away is so ridiculous, I can't help but laugh.

"Is this how it ends…?"

I've been killed. I got myself killed.

"I went through 27,753 repetitions of excruciating idleness, only to have it all end like this—what an utter waste of time. I admit, I'm…I'm exhausted."

To be completely accurate, I'm not dead yet, but whatever's left of me in the lump of blood and guts that once formed my body can see the writing on the wall. I'm dying. Well past the point of no return. Aya Otonashi killed me after all.

"Damn…! To think my prize would meet this fate after such a ridiculous amount of time… I've never cursed my own incompetence more than now!"

Aya Otonashi looks truly regretful as she mutters to herself.

"…Might as well drop this and try for another Box. There was nothing here. All I can do is look for the next one."

Her eyes don't see me. Actually, I'm sure they never once saw *me*, from the beginning of all this.

From the start up until the bitter end, this girl had eyes only for the Box supposedly hidden inside me.

So will none of this have ever occurred, either? No, I'm sure that's not the case. If the Box known as the Rejecting Classroom truly is inside me, then it'll be destroyed when I die, crushed just like my body against the truck.

There will be no more repetitions.

It's all so ironic. If this was the one and only means of putting an end to the Rejecting Classroom, then I should've just set out to die from the get-go. I can't get over the hollowness of it all. This world must've been some sort of purgatory for me.

But our battle is finally at an end.

It may have been completely one-sided, with no surprises or upsets, but it's over all the same.

Yeah, *that's what you believe, isn't it, Otonashi?*

I'm sorry. I truly am, Otonashi.

It's all because you ignored me for so long. If it weren't for that, I might not have made this mistake.

That's why we spent all this time in vain.

C'mon, Otonashi. It's so simple once you think about it. There's no way someone as mediocre as me could be the main character of all this.

I want to tell her, but there's no way of doing that any longer. I can't even open my mouth, much less speak.

My consciousness fades, and I drift off into death.

And then—nothing ends at all.

I'm in the place I can never remember once the dream ends.

I've received the Box from that person.

"Just relax. Of course, there are some risks involved in this kind of thing, but it's not what you're thinking of. You aren't going to lose something else you value, and it's not going to steal your life or soul. Actually, the reason anyone ends up with those negative side effects isn't necessarily an innate characteristic of the object, but rather the nature of the person using it. As long as you use it correctly, all it will do is grant your wish."

If I use it correctly...

I wonder if that requirement is actually as simple as it sounds. I have no idea. I don't know about any of that, but I do know this is an exceptional condition, even with all those risks attached. It's the same as receiving a lottery ticket certain to win. It's definitely possible that winning a huge sum of money could derail your life. But most people probably wouldn't consider that to be the risk.

That's why I ask if there are any people who don't accept the offer of the Box.

"Why do you ask that?"

Because someone is trying to reject it right now.

"Are you getting cold feet? Maybe you don't believe me? Or are you afraid of me?"

All those reasons are true, in a way, but that isn't really what this is about. All it boils down to is that I don't need it.

My wish is to continue in my average, ordinary life, and I already have that without using the Box.

It's like how someone with a trillion yen wouldn't care much about the idea of receiving a hundred million. I know it's valuable, which is precisely why I can't accept it from someone I know nothing about.

Yes, I know without a doubt that I returned the Box.

That's why…

…*even if I did wish for days of endless repetition to maintain the normalcy of my life, I am absolutely not the culprit.*

27, 753rd Time

Scritch, scritch, scritch, scritch—

What's that sound? It's so quiet, like you could completely miss it if you didn't listen carefully. But the sound is coming from within me, and I absolutely shouldn't ignore it.

Scritch, scritch, scritch, scritch.

It's like someone's using a tiny, tiny file, but what are they rasping away at? If the source of the sound is inside me, it has to be something within my body.

Scritch, scritch, scritch, scritch, scritch, scritch, scritch, scritch, scritch, scritch, scritch, scritch, scritch, scritch, scritch, scritch.

The sound is so small, but it seems like the loudest noise in the world, and I plug my ears out of instinct. Not even that keeps the insistent scratching at bay, though. That makes sense—actually, blocking my ears would make it easier to hear since it's inside me. That's why I can't block the sound. I can't escape hearing myself wearing away.

It hurts, too. Being filed down is definitely painful. This is what it would feel like if my heart turned into a porcupine fish. A constant prickling sensation. Is it guilt? I thought that would be the first thing to go, but it's proving unexpectedly persistent.

Scritch, scritch, scritch, scritch, scritch, scritch, scritch, scritch, scritch, scritch, scritch, scritch, scritch, scritch, scritch, scritch.

I'm being whittled away.

My heart.

All of who I am.

I'm losing my shape, becoming a handful of sawdust. No, that isn't right. I'm already...far beyond that point. I'm already nothing but dust.

After twenty thousand repetitions, I'm no longer who I used to be. I know that. Unable to bear the tedium, my heart has slipped away. I can't communicate meaningfully with others anymore.

This world is rejecting me.

That's to be expected. I never belonged here to begin with, and I forced my way in. The classroom where everyone else exists has rejected me each time.

The only thing I know for certain is how to make all of this better.

But I will never, under any circumstances, do that.

After all, my wish hasn't been granted yet.

...Wait. I thought I was already nothing but dust. Why is my wish still here, untouched? Is that even possible? It should have been ground down along with my heart and everything else that I am because, to tell the truth—

—I can't even remember what I actually wished for anymore.

"Ha-ha-ha."

I can't stop myself from laughing. That's right. I can't remember. Ha-ha-ha, I can't remember. What did I wish for again? Hey, help me remember. Ha-ha-ha, don't play around with me like this. Why did I torture myself by going through each repetition? All I can do is laugh. It's all I can do, and yet I've even forgotten how. I'm just forcing the sounds through my expressionless face.

If this is how it's going to be, then let's just end it.

It's the simplest conclusion. Why didn't I think of that sooner?

I should just kill him. That's right—I should just end his life. I should kill *Kazuki Hoshino*. He's the source of all my suffering, after all. If it would put an end to the pain, I should just finish him off right now.

But somewhere deep within me, I know: The fetter that was once my wish will never let any of this end for me...

5,000th Time

0th Time

1st Time

1 0, 0 0

9,000th Time

8,000th Time

7,000th Time

27,754th Time

Before long, my body is cold and empty. This means my very being should be hollow, too, but for some reason I wake up as usual.

The chill should have vanished by now, but it's still here. Unable to bear it, I wrap my arms around myself as I shiver in my bed.

I was killed.

It's March 2, during a loop somewhere up in the tens of thousands.

So even if something kills me, the Rejecting Classroom continues on as ever before. This realization seems to be carving me away from the inside, ensuring that the cold will never leave me.

I can't take staying still like that any longer, so I head straight to school without bothering to really eat anything.

Outside is the overcast sky I know so well now. It'll rain tomorrow. How long has it been since I last saw the sun?

The classroom is empty. I guess it makes sense since I'm at least an hour early for our first class.

A question pops into my head: Why am I so diligent about going to school?

I've noticed the repetition of the Rejecting Classroom many times before, like I did just now. If so, couldn't I try not going to school as a way of fighting back against the cycle?

But no, I always go. Of course I do. As long as I'm in good shape,

I'll go. It's part of my regular everyday life. It's such an obvious, established fact that I would never even think of changing my routine. If it means maintaining the normalcy of my life, I'll resist a new pattern at any cost. It's my one true conviction.

I can see that now. That's probably why I'm here. None of it makes the slightest shred of sense, but that's what I feel in my gut. I'll go to class even if no one's there.

"…"

I move to the center of the classroom and climb on top of someone's desk, my outdoor shoes still on. Sorry, whoever sits there. I try to remember their name or even their face, but I can't. I'm sorry. I truly am.

I survey the room. I know that standing on the desk won't change anything, but there's still no one to be seen in the gloom of the classroom.

There's no one in the classroom.

There's no one in the classroom.

"……It's so cold."

I wrap my arms around my body.

I hear the door open. Seeing me standing atop someone's desk, the new arrival frowns.

"…What the hell are you doing, Kazu?"

Daiya gives me a strange look.

I can feel the tension bleed away from my face.

"……Man, that's a relief."

Whispering this, I slowly climb down off the desk. Daiya watches me the entire time, his face scrunched in a scowl.

"Seeing you really takes a load off my mind, Daiya."

"That's nice."

"I mean, I know you're the real thing."

"…C'mon, Kazu, you're starting to scare me here, and it's been a long time since that happened."

"You may be real, but everything else here is fake. I can't share anything with you. The next Daiya I meet won't know the me who is here now. It's like this is all some show, and I'm the only one on the other side of the TV screen. I know about you, but you don't know about me. If that's true, can I really even say you exist?"

That's why there's no one here.

No one?

"Oh..."

That's wrong.

There is one person here.

A single, solitary entity who can share memories with me. As long as I don't neglect to carry my memories over, I'll never be separated from her.

It's all clear to me now. It's always been just the two of us here in the Rejecting Classroom. She's been beside me all along within the cramped confines of this space that I will neither escape nor try to. She's always viewed me as an enemy, so I've never had a chance to think about it before.

I sit down in my seat.

She sits down in hers next to me.

I can't believe it. Just imagining her sitting beside me makes me feel a little better. Even though she's the one who killed me.

Is that why?

Why? Why what? I don't understand. I can't make sense of my emotions. But the warmth is still draining away from my body. Rapidly. The temperature of my chilly flesh will drop to zero. It'll freeze and freeze, agonizingly, until I can't move a muscle.

"My name is Aya Otonashi. Pleased to meet you."

The "transfer student" blushed and smiled slightly, as if she really were a transfer student.

"......What...?"

I didn't understand.

No, actually, I did.

"I am just as firmly trapped here as the rest of you. If I decide to stop remembering and give up, I'll go through all of this over and over with no meaning just like everyone else. It would be as simple as spilling a cup of water balanced on top of my head."

A voice I'm sure I've heard before repeats these words like a refrain.

I look at the girl on the podium. I examine her features, trying to make sure she's real. She can't be anything but real, even though there's no way she could be, either.

Is she Aya Otonashi?

That's impossible. She'd never give up, not even if all her efforts over these twenty-thousand-plus transfers turned out to be pointless, not even if she realized that the culprit she had been pursuing for so long wasn't, in fact, me. She'd never give up! Never!

This isn't like her at all.

Fully half of the class has been rejected. Nobody notices, though, as the class continues to barrage her with questions. Her replies are curt, but she's answering all the same, with none of her usual disdain.

She's just like a regular transfer student.

This scene shouldn't exist in reality. It's a fictitious event, a lie. All of it is a lie. So does that mean Aya Otonashi is a lie, too?

That's...

That's...

"Unacceptable."

Someone else might think so, but I won't allow it.

I won't let Aya Otonashi become a fake.

"...Is something wrong, Hoshino?"

Why is my teacher asking me this?

Probably because I've suddenly leaped to my feet.

I quickly glance back at Mogi for a second. All eyes in the classroom are on me, including hers. Her face is as blank as ever, though, so there's no telling what she's thinking.

If you ask her opinion on my behavior, I can guarantee she won't have an answer for you. We've been in the classroom together for a long time, but that's the extent of our relationship.

The only chance for us to become more than just classmates would arrive tomorrow.

So, yeah—there's no Mogi here.

No one is here.

That's why...nothing matters.

Any classmates who would forget my strange behavior—*I've cut them out.*

I only have eyes for Otonashi. I walk up to the platform where she stands. What I'm about to do now is something I would normally never do, on the same level as confessing my feelings to Mogi.

I stop directly in front of Otonashi.

Unperturbed, she regards me with a serious expression, as if she's sizing me up. It's like she's seeing me for the first time, and it's infuriating.

"Hey, Hoshino! What are you doing?"

Mr. Kokubo sounds calm, but I can tell my behavior is disturbing him. My classmates are all muttering similar things.

I ignore everything and drop to one knee before the girl I used to think was my enemy. I lower my head and extend my hand to her.

"What is this about?" she asks.

Her tone is so polite. She would normally never speak to me this way.

"Your escort has arrived."

If this is how it's going to be, then I have no choice but to play the part.

"...Wh-what did you say?"

"Your escort has arrived, Princess Maria. It is I, Hathaway, the one who has sworn to betray everything, to turn all and sundry against him as he stands alone in your defense."

Oddly enough, the hubbub around us fades. That makes sense. If I'm going to bring Otonashi back, I have to make her see that nothing around us exists. So this situation is easy to understand.

My head still bowed, I wait for Aya Otonashi to take my hand and beckon me to my feet. I wait for her to make me dance upon her palm.

But none of that happens.

Aya Otonashi's hand never takes mine.

Instead, a loud *clonk* fills my head with a dull ringing, and I fall to the side.

"...What a creep."

My head was lowered, so I have no idea what caused the impact. I finally understand what happened when I look up at Otonashi from the floor. Her right knee gave me a good whack to the side of the head.

Yeah, okay. That makes sense. I must've been dreaming to think Otonashi would ever reach out to me.

"Heh…"

If she truly is Aya Otonashi, beyond a shadow of a doubt, *then she would never extend her hand or show me the slightest inkling of kindness.*

"Heh, heh-heh-heh…"

Otonashi is laughing, as if unable to hold in her amusement at the situation any longer. I don't think I've seen anything like this once in the twenty thousand times we've repeated all this.

I'm still laid out, and my head still hurts, but I can feel the tension in my face relax along with my mind.

"You certainly took your time, my beloved Hathaway. How dare you make a maiden such as me, whose only virtue is to faithfully await your arrival by the window, who is so delicate that she has never held anything heavier than a spoon, wait for so long? I never thought in these 27,753 times that I would be thrust into the battlefield alone."

Otonashi stoops down and reaches toward me.

She grasps my wrist as I start to stand and yanks me to my feet.

Yeah, this feels right.

This is the Aya Otonashi I know.

"…My strength is greater than ever before, thanks to you."

Otonashi's eyes widen, as if that caught her off guard. The corners of her mouth twitch upward again.

"Well, your skill with words has certainly improved, Hathaway!"

Keeping her grip on my wrist, she leads me from the classroom.

She pulls me away, ignoring homeroom, the teacher, the students—ignoring everything that I cut out and cast aside.

After dragging me from the classroom, she set me on the rear seat of a large motorcycle, with no helmet. I'm freaking out now because I've never experienced speeds like this before, so I'm clinging to Otonashi's surprisingly slender waist. (Well, actually, it feels just the way it looks, but I can't help but perceive her as more substantial.) When I ask her in a shaky voice if she has a license, she calmly states that of course she doesn't.

"I picked it up during all the extra time I've had in my lifetime of transfers. Pretty worthwhile, don't you think?"

She does seem to have a knack for driving. I have to give her that.

I ask her whether she's acquired any other skills along the way, and her reply is simply "Of course." She can drive a car, too, as I predicted, but she's also tried her hand at martial arts, sports, languages, music, and pretty much everything else possible within the confines of the Rejecting Classroom's repetitions. By this point, she can score near-perfect marks on university admissions exams. She claims she could already score 90 percent on those before the transfers started, though.

Otonashi was a high-caliber individual to begin with, of course, but these 27,754 transfers have given her that much more time to spend improving herself. I can't do the arithmetic, but if you convert all those loops into days, they add up to around seventy-six years. A person's birth and death could occur in that span of time. It's really amazing when you think about it.

"Hey, Otonashi, you're the same age as me, right?"

Perhaps because of that line of thought, I'm curious about her actual age.

"...No, I'm not."

"Huh? So then how old are you?"

"What does it matter?"

Otonashi sounds unhappy as she replies. Maybe she doesn't want to talk about it. I've always heard it's rude to ask a woman's age, so maybe she's at the point where it's impolite to ask.

When I think long and hard about it, no one in my grade should be as mature as Otonashi is. She's my classmate only because the role of a transfer student is convenient for infiltrating the Rejecting Classroom. Otonashi could be old enough that wearing a school uniform is more like cosplay for her.

"Hoshino, if there are any inappropriate thoughts running through that head of yours, I'll knock you off this bike right here and now."

She's awfully perceptive for someone with her eyes on the road.

"So, um, anyway, you learned how to ride a motorcycle only during all your transfers, right? That means this bike probably wasn't yours to begin with. Who's the owner? Your dad, maybe?"

I don't know much about motorcycles, but this doesn't seem like the model a lady would ride.

"I don't know."

"...Huh?"

"Pretty careless to leave your keys in your bike while it's just sitting outside your house, don't you think?"

I can't argue with that, but does that mean she...?

"Chain locks are easy to break if you have the right tools. This bike is always in the same state every time I transfer. To no one's surprise."

I decide not to press the topic any further. I don't know anything at all. Nope, nothing at all.

"If you lose your memory, will you forget how to drive, along with all the other skills and knowledge you've picked up?"

That would be such a huge waste.

"..."

She doesn't answer.

"Otonashi?"

Still nothing. Maybe...

"Were you also thinking it would be a big waste, Otonashi?"

Maybe the skills and know-how she seems to have picked up at random aren't all just to kill the time. Not even Otonashi would relish the thought of parting with all these talents. That's why she doesn't want to lose her memory.

She pushed herself to master these skills in order to create that reluctance.

And in that case...

It takes a while, but my train of thought finally arrives at the real question:

Why did Otonashi pretend to forget everything?

*　　*　　*

Our destination is a hotel that, while I wouldn't exactly call it first-rate, is the most expensive place around here and definitely beyond the means of any high school student.

After checking in with well-practiced ease, Otonashi turns down the bellboy's offer to show us the way and sets off without a moment's hesitation.

She plops down on the sofa as soon as we're in the room.

I sit down on the bed, trying to keep my excitement at being in a luxury hotel in check.

When I think about it, it's crazy that I'm here alone in a hotel room with a woman. But that woman happens to be Otonashi, so it doesn't really feel like that kind of situation. In fact, I'm not nervous at all.

"I should've figured you'd be rich, too. Or at least you kinda seemed like you would be."

"Whether I'm wealthy or not doesn't matter. All the money I spend returns to me with each transfer anyway."

"...Now that you mention it, that's true. That means I could go buy every single Umaibo in the convenience store. Awesome!"

"Who cares? We didn't come here to talk about trivial matters like snacks, did we?"

"N-no, you're right. What exactly do we need to talk about?"

"The direction we're going to take from here on out. Now that my theory that you were the one responsible for all this has collapsed, I'm lost at sea here."

"Sorry about that."

"Spare me your sarcasm."

I wasn't trying to be sarcastic.

"So why not find out who the real culprit is? I know that's easier said than done, but it seems like losing this preconception that I'm the one responsible is a major development."

"...Hoshino, I've transferred 27,754 times now. Do you understand that?"

"...What do you mean?"

"We talked a bit about this last time. Even if I did wrongly assume you were the culprit, that doesn't mean I stopped suspecting other people. When I interacted with other possible leads, I always kept the idea that I could be wrong in the forefront of my mind... The fact that I misidentified you as my target only shows that I was still careless, of course."

"So you didn't find anyone else as suspicious as I was?"

"That's right. I've been at this over and over for 27,754 times. The only one who wouldn't show their true colors in all that time would have to be the owner of the Box."

"Hmm, do you think maybe you were too obvious in your searching, and they figured out you were after them?"

"It's still not possible. Even if they were on guard, we're talking about 27,754 times through the cycle here. Are you saying the owner has the smarts and endurance to stay hidden for all that time? Well, the bottom line is I still haven't been able to find them. Dammit, why? The owner of the Box has to be one of the people who is in the classroom."

"...Hold on a minute. You're saying that the culprit has to be in the classroom? It absolutely has to be one of our classmates?"

Now that I think about it, Otonashi did mention last time that there weren't many suspects.

"No, any teachers and students from other classes who come into room 1-6 are also suspects. As the name suggests, the Rejecting Classroom encompasses exclusively classroom 1-6. The only people caught in this are those who entered that area between March second and March third."

"......? Then why can I leave the classroom and see other people?"

"I can tell by your face that you don't get it. Hoshino, *do you really think it's possible to rewind time?*"

"Um..."

What is she getting at? If you deny that idea, then the whole premise of the Rejecting Classroom collapses.

"...But it's the Box that makes all that possible, right?"

"Correct. It's possible as long as the Box is there. But what I'm asking here is your opinion. Do you truly believe that having something like the Box would allow time to be rewound at all? Do you believe the phenomenon is possible to begin with?"

I have no clue what Otonashi's trying to tell me.

"I..."

All I can do is give my honest answer to her questions, without worrying too much about the meaning behind them.

"I think that nothing will change what's already occurred."

I've wished more times than I can count that I could reverse time. But I don't think I'd believe in time travel even if time machines were real. Even if I hopped back to the past, I don't think I would believe it until I saw undeniable proof. Maybe my doubts would persist no matter what sort of proof was presented to me.

I'm not sure if that's the answer she's looking for, but Otonashi nods her head with a *hmm*.

"I think your understanding of things may be normal. Perhaps the one who made the Rejecting Classroom sees things the same way you do."

"What are you saying?"

"The Box granted their wish to its fullest extent. Completely, to the last little detail. In other words, when it granted the owner's wish, *the Box included their inability to believe it's possible to rewind time.* Do you understand what I'm saying?"

"Um..."

You want to reverse time. But at the same time, you don't think it's possible. The attempt to reconcile these views probably twists the wish. That's something I can get my head around.

"So do you think you're actually being returned to the past?"

"Hoshino, have I ever once expressed this situation as 'being returned to the past'?"

I'm not sure, mostly because I've lost almost all my memories of the time I spent with Otonashi.

"I'll keep this short. If the Rejecting Classroom was born from someone's wish to rewind time, it's a sorry attempt. A work of inferior quality—defective."

"Okay, then why have you experienced all of this over twenty thousand times?"

"Hmph. Well, that in itself is proof of how broken the classroom is. If time were being rewound perfectly, there's no reason my memories should be so precisely excluded from what it's targeting. And even before that, if the repetition is so perfect, why was someone like me who wasn't originally part of the class able to infiltrate it as a transfer student?"

Otonashi gives me a sidelong glance.

"Knowing you, your thought process probably led you to some cheap notion that anything is possible for me."

Well, she has me there. No arguing that.

"In short, all I did was sneak inside the Box. I didn't intend to be treated as a transfer student, for instance. That's just the role the culprit gave me. The setting of the Rejecting Classroom is room 1-6, so my being a transfer student was the most natural explanation for the sudden appearance of a newcomer who's roughly the same age as the students. Basically, the culprit's sense of balance found a way to keep things plausible."

"...?"

I don't really get what she means. *Keep things plausible?* What does that have to do with anything?

"Ugh, why are you always so slow on the uptake? Fine, let's frame it this way: Say the Rejecting Classroom is a movie directed by the culprit. All the filming is done, so all that's left is the editing. But then, all of a sudden, the director gets word from the producers that there's an actor they absolutely have to have in the film for commercial reasons. All the parts have already been cast, but the director can't just stick the actor on the screen without giving them a role. It would derail the entire production. So the director makes the most minimal of rewrites possible to the screenplay and assigns the actor a part. And that's how I was made into a transfer student to keep things logical."

"In other words, the culprit couldn't keep you from getting into the classroom, so they had to find some way to make you a part of it. They were forced to make you into a sudden transfer student and put together your life for March second. Is that what you mean?"

"Exactly. But even then there was still something off about my presence in the Rejecting Classroom, right? It's a pain to explain every little detail, so I'll just jump to the conclusion. This is not reality. Nothing is repeating itself. It's just a small, isolated space. *This is all an ill-conceived* 'wish' that will continue to exist as long as a single person, even the culprit, believes that time is looping."

"Uh...and that's why you were saying that the loop is imperfect?"

"Yes. The one who made the wish doesn't believe that time can turn back; all they're doing is refusing to let time move forward. They're rejecting it. All the owner of the Box needs to do is continue pulling the wool over their own eyes."

"Does that flaw also explain why you and I can keep our memories?"

"Most likely. Our respective reasons for the ability could be different, but I have no doubt that they're due to the defects of the Rejecting Classroom."

There's one thing I still can't get my head around.

"So just who are you?"

Otonashi's displeasure is obvious. I guess she didn't want to hear that.

"Ah, well...I mean, you don't have to answer if you don't want to, but..."

Though the scowl never leaves her face, she opens her mouth to speak.

"I don't have some sort of easy-to-understand title like you're hoping for. 'I'm just a student'...is what I would like to say, but I suppose that label hasn't really applied since a year ago. So what is my role...? I've never really given it a name, but there's probably only one way to put it. I am..."

Otonashi spits out the next words as if it genuinely pains her to do so.

"...a Box."

"You're a Box? What do you mean?"

Her brows furrow even more when I parrot her answer back to her in confusion.

"There are certain things that prevent me from explaining in more detail, so I can't say any more than that."

I guess it's obvious I'm not pleased about her inability to clarify, because Otonashi continues speaking after glancing at me.

"But I can tell you this. I have obtained and used a Box in the past."

"Whaaat?!!"

"That, and *my wish is still being granted*."

So Otonashi has a Box, too?

"I'm sure you must be curious as to why I'm still looking for a Box if I already have one. That's fine. I'll tell you. My wish was certainly granted. But at the same time, I lost everything."

"What do you mean, 'everything'?"

"My family, my friends, my classmates, my relatives, my teachers, my neighbors, the people I was close to—I lost all of them thanks to my wish. Everyone who was ever involved with me is gone."

I'm speechless.

"You mean that…literally, right? Not just some figure of speech?"

"That's right. And I can't just let things stay where they are. That's what keeps me moving."

Otonashi has lost everything. She has nothing more to fear. Perhaps that's why she's so focused and bold.

Exactly what "wish" did Otonashi put in the Box that would leave her in this state?

"Is there any way you can break that Box? If you break it, won't that negate the wish?"

"Hoshino."

A hint of warning creeps into Otonashi's tone as she replies to my natural question.

"The Box is still granting my wish, understand? Don't make me say any more than that."

I get it. Of course Otonashi considered that some question like this might pop into my head.

Basically, the Box took everything from Otonashi. But *that still wasn't enough to make her want to negate its wish.*

While I silently mull this over, Otonashi pulls herself together and resumes the conversation.

"My wish and the wish of the owner of the Rejecting Classroom are incompatible with each other. That's just the way Boxes work. So now that I've come in here, I fight back to reduce its ability to get in my way. But I should stress that all I'm doing is lessening it. Put another way, not even I can completely avoid the influence of the Rejecting Classroom. I'm not sure just how much it's affected me. If I succumb to it, I could end up trapped here myself... But I get the feeling I told you that a long time ago."

If everything she's saying is true, then what does the owner of the Rejecting Classroom think about Otonashi? I have a hard time believing it's anything good.

"Anyway, it seems you've managed to digest all of that, so let's get back to the matter at hand. It's probably impossible to obtain and use the Rejecting Classroom at this point. The owner has already expended its power. That's why all we need to worry about is putting an end to it."

"And how can we do that?"

"We'd have to tear the Box away from the culprit. Or perhaps crush them. That's about it. However, if we can find the one who gives out the Boxes, we may be able to convince them to do something. They're not likely to be inside with us, though, so that isn't a realistic option."

The one who gives out the Boxes?

I'm about to ask more but then decide not to.

Even though I've met ★, it's like I don't know about them, nor do I want to.

"......Basically, we have to find the one behind all this before we can get anywhere, correct?"

"Oh? 'Get anywhere,' you say? Are you trying to tell me you think everything until now was completely meaningless? That it was an unproductive waste of time? You've got a lot of nerve."

"N-no, I was just asking..."

"Hmph. So then I guess you mean to tell me your knowledge and quick wits could be the key to solving these riddles I couldn't handle on my own. Don't tell me that you said what you did without a single idea in your head?"

"...Ungh..."

I wince. I don't have any breakthroughs.

"If you understand that, then you should also understand that there is no reason why I can't find the owner. But there is one thing... Unlike others, the owner isn't allowed to die within the Rejecting Classroom. My life has ended countless times in the classroom, yet I'm still here, and I haven't lost my Box."

"It's different for the owner, though?"

"Yeah. Owners and their Boxes are connected. The instant the owner of this Box dies, the Rejecting Classroom will collapse. I've confirmed this in several similar instances, so I'm sure it's true. The Box is destroyed at the moment of its owner's death. This would also cause the special nature of the Rejecting Classroom to disappear, and the concept of death would be restored."

"And that would cause the owner to die as normal...?"

"Correct."

"That means we can say for sure that I'm not the one behind this. And of course you aren't, either."

"Right."

That also means Mogi isn't on the list of suspects. She's died in the accident plenty of times before.

"...So what about our missing classmates? Do you think that has anything to do with death?"

"I'm not certain, but I don't think it does. It's probably another feature of the Rejecting Classroom, though I can't really guess why it's there."

Hold on a second.

I suddenly realize something—a way to easily identify the person at the root of it all. The blood drains from my face. What am I thinking?! It's too hideous to even consider. But, but...

Aya Otonashi could do it.

I can't bring myself to voice the thought aloud. At the same time, I'm surprised that she hasn't already come up with the idea herself. There's no way she wouldn't have thought of this. Then why hasn't she tried it? Could it be that...?

"Hoshino."

I jerk back to attention at the sound of my name.

"What are you thinking about? Don't tell me you've come up with some means of uncovering the owner?"

My body twitches again.

"You did think of something, didn't you...?"

"Uh, no, I—"

"It's no use trying to fool me. Don't forget how much time I've spent with you. I was on your tail for longer than I was on anyone else's here. Not that I wanted to be."

I know that. You don't need Otonashi's sharp instincts to tell that I'm trying to hide something.

"..."

That doesn't make my idea any easier to put into words, though.

"Even someone as slow as you should know by now that I'm not the most patient of people, Hoshino."

I'm not dealing with someone who'd buy any old lie. Once I open my mouth, she'll get the truth out of me in the end, no matter how much I try to avoid it.

But still...

"Hoshino!!"

Otonashi grabs me by the collar. It hurts. Like, seriously. Of course it does. This girl willingly suffered repeating a day more than twenty thousand times just to get the Box.

"Say it! Tell me your idea!!"

I know I'll regret it if I do. But can I really keep my mouth shut under these circumstances?

That's why I voice my idea in the end.

"We need to kill all our classmates."

It's that simple. If dying even once eliminates someone as a possible suspect, then that's what needs to happen. We have to kill them all. That's the simple, reprehensible truth.

Everyone who dies in here comes back to life, though, so there's really nothing to worry about. I could never be so cut-and-dried about it, but I'm sure Otonashi could.

She's created tons of corpses to help her hold on to her memories, after all.

I'm still curious as to whether this hasn't crossed her mind before, though. Why hasn't she stumbled upon this strategy not just to retain her memory, but also as a means of narrowing down the list of suspects? Why wouldn't she choose to implement an efficient strategy that could've ended this in just forty or so times?

No response.

No reaction.

I slowly raise my eyes to look at her face.

With a tight hold on my collar, she's regarding me with an unblinking stare.

"That..." Otonashi quietly releases her grip. "That's not a strategy at all."

"...What?"

"That's like human experimentation. The best way to test the effects of something on the body is to use a human subject, but the method should never even be an option," Otonashi softly whispers, never looking away from me. "Why? The answer is simple: because it's inhumane. The moment you do something like that, you can no longer call yourself a human being... Ah well, I am a Box, after all. Maybe that's why. Maybe that's why you..." There is pure, undiluted rage boiling in her eyes. "You don't think of me as a human!"

I can understand her anger. I'd probably feel the same way if someone viewed me like that. It was a thoughtless thing to say.

All the same, I still don't get it.

"But didn't you kill people to make sure your memories carried over?"

"......What're you saying?" Otonashi shoots me a sharp look, as if she finds the accusation unbearable.

"...Y-you created scenes that would burn themselves into your mind in order to hang on to your memory."

"I've had enough of your insults! I thought I just explained this. I can resist the effects of the Rejecting Classroom because I'm a Box!"

She's right. The idea that she was killing others to retain her memories was just Daiya's hypothesis.

But even that isn't enough for me to accept what happened.

"Why are you making that face? If you've got something to say, say it!"

Otonashi seizes me by the collar again.

This time I meet her angry glare with one of my own.

It isn't like I was working myself up to do this. I didn't even consider the implications of doing something so unlike myself as glaring back at her.

I'm in the palm of Otonashi's hand. I know that much, and that's exactly why I'm here talking with her like this now.

But my next words wrecked that:

"If you care so much about human lives, then why did you kill me?!"

And that's when all words between us are lost.

After that fateful accusation, things didn't return to normal between Otonashi and me.

She had no retort for me, not even an angry look. I was nonexistent to her. Naturally, I was as powerless before her as always, so my only recourse was to leave the hotel.

I've been loitering out front for a little while, but that's nothing more than my lingering emotions. Just wasting time. Glancing out of the corner of my eye at the bike Otonashi "borrowed" from somebody, I start walking. I stop by a convenience store and buy a bottle of tea. I sip on it for a while, and by the time it's empty, I realize I can't really recall what I was drinking.

This could be the end.

Unlike Otonashi, I have no idea whether my memories will stay with me next time. If she no longer has any use for me, I'll eventually forget everything and be expelled from the Rejecting Classroom. I'll disappear like all the others.

The road is silent. There are no streetlights. No color at all.

It's like the person who made this world didn't bother to fill in all the details.

I raise the empty bottle to my lips. It's like if I don't pretend to drink, I'll be swallowed myself... What is it? I can't pinpoint what's bothering me.

Suddenly, I can hear the music of my favorite band in the quiet street. What's going on? Oh, that's just my ringtone... My ringtone? Does that mean someone's calling me? Oh yeah, that's right!

I don't remember doing it, but I must have given her my number, maybe in one of the other worlds.

I pull my cell phone out of my pocket.

The caller ID on the screen reads "Kokone Kirino."

I look up at the sky. I know things never work out that easily, but it doesn't hurt to hope.

I take a breath to compose myself and then answer the phone.

"Oh, hey, Kazu."

I could be wrong, but I can't detect the usual energy in Kokone's voice. Maybe she's always like this on the phone? We're friends and all, but I've never really had a phone conversation with her before.

"Um, hey…"

I have the feeling I know where this is going. Yeah, I'm sure of it. I just can't remember it all right now.

"Can you come meet me somewhere?"

What is it? What happens next?

"There's something I have to tell you, Kazu."

3,087th Time

It's a fact that I love Umaibo, but I'm actually not a huge fan of the teriyaki burger flavor.

We're in the run-down park in front of her house, talking in front of the fountain. I'm eating the Umaibo she gave me.

"…So what do you think?"

"……Hmm, uh, I guess it's not too bad."

"I wasn't asking about your snack."

I know that, but my mind is racing too much to answer anything else.

"…Will you go out with me, then?"

My experiences in love have been so few that even that question doesn't freak me out as much as it should.

Either way, my classmate is probably just as nervous as I am. I've never seen her like this before.

Her eyes are always large, but they seem especially so now. Maybe it's the new mascara she tried this morning. She's watching me intently.

I can't help but look away.

At a loss for what to do, I feel like I have to say something. "So…I guess that means you like me?"

The face of the girl before me turns bright red.

"…I think so."

"You think so?" I repeat her words as a question without thinking.

"……Wh-why would you ask me that? You know what my answer is… O-or do you just want to hear me say it?"

"Ah…!" I lower my eyes as I finally realize how insensitive that was. "I'm sorry."

I apologize by reflex. She meets my gaze through her lashes and whispers:

"…Yes, I like you."

She's so adorable in that moment that I break eye contact. The affection radiating from her is melting my heart. It doesn't hurt that she's good-looking, too.

She's so cheerful and always has a crowd around her. I know she's turned down more than a few suitors, too. I would probably really enjoy going out with her, but…

"I'm sorry."

But that's my response. I'm surprised at how easily I could say that. I know I'm passing up a great opportunity. It's just that I can't see myself going out with her. It wouldn't feel real.

The hope in her eyes disappears, and tears replace it. I can't make myself look, even though I know I'm the one responsible.

I can't find the words. If I open my mouth, the only thing that'll come out is "Sorry."

"……It was hard for you to say, wasn't it?"

I nod at her hushed words.

"…Hey, you like Umaibo, right?"

I nod at that, too, despite the lack of context.

"You aren't such a big fan of the teriyaki burger flavor, though."

"…Yeah."

"Which one's your favorite?"

"Um…maybe corn potage?" I answer unsteadily, unable to figure out why she's asking me this.

"I see. I see, I see…"

Her head bobs in time with her words.

"Ha-ha, *I guess I failed.*"

There's nothing special about her remark, but for some reason I can't get over it. Like how shoddy editing in a video sticks out like a sore thumb.

"So maybe if I'd made a move on you differently, you might've gone out with me?"

She keeps her head low as she says this.

I'm not so sure I would have. My thoughts are so conflicted... On second thought, no. I know what I would've done.

I would've turned her down, no matter what.

And my answer will never change, as long as it's the same me and the same circumstances.

As long as it's today, I can never imagine myself dating her. *As long as it's today,* I'll always turn her down.

"That look on your face says you're not so sure."

I can't say anything in response to that.

She takes my silence as a yes and finally gives a little smile.

"Okay, I get it. *I'll just keep after you until you finally return my feelings.*"

Maybe it's not a bad idea. That's the least I can give her after turning her down so bluntly.

Still—it won't work if it's any day before tomorrow.

27,754th Time

After everything imploded between Otonashi and me, not to mention my unexpected summons from Kokone, I'm thoroughly spent... That's just an excuse, though.

The truth is that I completely forgot.

There's an accident that always occurs at this intersection, like clockwork.

I'm in no danger myself. The shock of dying was enough that the collision now instantly surfaces in my mind like a conditioned response as soon as I approach the intersection. Keeping myself out of danger isn't an issue.

That alone isn't enough to guarantee that disaster won't strike, though. Assuming the accident here is inevitable, all it means is that the truck will hit someone else.

That's what always escapes me, and that's why I'm unable to save anyone. Even though I know someone will be hurt, I've never prevented it. Forgetfulness is the cheapest of excuses.

I'm absolute scum. *I might as well be killing the victim myself.*

Kasumi Mogi is at the intersection.

The girl I like.

The truck comes barreling down the road as it always does.

It's impossible to do anything for her from where I stand. No matter how fast I run, I'll never close that distance in time.

She'll end up covered in blood. The girl I like will become a bloody mess. And it'll happen because of me.

Again and again, I'll watch it happen; again and again, the girl I like will be dyed in red. Again and again, it'll be my fault.

"AAAAAAAHHHH!!"

I sprint toward the truck. Am I doing it to try and save Mogi? No. That isn't it at all. I'm just pretending to do something so I can satisfy my guilty conscience with the claim that I tried.

I'm scum, the lowest of the low.

And then I watch it happen.

"Huh…?"

The girl I have no chance of saving is pushed out of the way of the truck.

It isn't me.

She's always too far for me to reach, even at my most frantic.

There's only one person who could.

The girl who always struggles on alone as I cast aside my memories and pretend not to know.

She'll never make it. She'll never have time to save herself.

All the same, Aya Otonashi runs out to save Mogi.

There it is. Now I remember.

I've witnessed this very scene many times before.

Things are always repeating themselves, anyway. Even Mogi's survival will fade into nothingness. All that remains is a memory nearly as painful as dying, the fear of witnessing death right before my eyes, and the despair of knowing that all of this will occur again and again.

Despite everything, Aya Otonashi leaps in front of the truck to save whoever who will be hit that day, over and over and over again.

I understand now.

How could I have forgotten this?

There's the sound of heavy impact and a deafening crash as the truck continues along its course and plows through the wall along the road.

The cacophony threatens to overwhelm me, but I still manage to make my way to Otonashi. Next to her, Mogi lies stiff as a board right where she landed, her expression blank in shock.

I look at Otonashi.

Her left leg is twisted at an impossible angle.

She's covered in a thick sweat, and as she sees me, she speaks with an expression so brave one would hardly suspect she was injured.

"I killed you last time." Her words are clear and precise, though it must be torture for her to speak. "I thought this would end if I killed the owner of the Box. I was wrong. But at the time, I believed that what I was doing was the only way to escape from the Rejecting Classroom. I thought I was doing the right thing, because once I got out of the classroom, I would reset, and the me who was forced to such inhuman extremes would disappear."

Everything finally falls into place. I know why Otonashi pretended to forget everything this time.

She lost all respect for herself.

She couldn't forgive herself for thinking it was okay if I died when I had my accident.

Her guilt was enough to make her cast aside the goal of obtaining the Box that kept her going for so long, and even the thought of escaping the Rejecting Classroom.

It was enough that she couldn't fight back when I screamed:

"If you care so much about human lives, then why did you kill me?!"

How could I have said such a horrible thing to her, especially when I had no basis for it?

Last time, I dashed out to save Mogi and ended up dying in the accident. Just as I assumed Otonashi was in essence murdering Mogi with the truck, I assumed she had killed me. I held on to this assumption, and it became why I said what I did. I should have known from the moment she vehemently denied the very thought of murdering our classmates. The truth was only that she arrived too late to save my life.

For some reason, this accident is unavoidable. Someone is always inevitably hit by the truck, and it just happened to be me that time.

"Heh, it's all so laughable. My crimes wouldn't vanish just because I forgot them. The Rejecting Classroom didn't vanish, and I now have no choice but to live with myself knowing how low I sank. Not even poetic justice is enough for this."

She coughs up a bit of blood as she finishes her last words.

"Otonashi, if you're in pain, you shouldn't talk…"

"But when else will I get the chance? I'm used to the pain. It all depends on how you think about it. I'd rather experience temporary pain like this than the long, drawn out agony of a chronic illness."

I don't think anyone can say they've "gotten used to" getting hit by a truck.

"I didn't lose my memory or escape from the Rejecting Classroom. Heh-heh, I feel like I already knew that, though. That I would never be released."

"…Why?"

"It's so simple. I know exactly why. My obsession won't let go of me that easily."

Otonashi struggles unsteadily to her feet. She should've stayed where she was, but I get the feeling she can't stand me looking down on her.

Her left leg is completely useless. She doubles over in a coughing fit, spitting up blood. But once she's able to lean against the guardrail for support, she seems to stand as tall as ever, watching me all the while.

Maybe because of Otonashi's movement, Mogi stirs from where she was lying in frozen, blank-faced shock. She looks over at me fearfully.

"…Mogi, are you all right?"

"……Eek!"

She screams as if she's remembering what happened.

"Wh-what were you two just talking about...? Not just now, since yesterday. Who are you?"

...What? Who is she looking at like that? Who would fill her eyes with such terror?

...I already know. She's looking at me.

I can't bear to see her so frightened, and instinctively, I reach out to cup her face with my hand.

"D-don't touch me!!"

Of course... What was I thinking? It's obviously me she's scared of, so what did I think trying to touch her would do? Did I really think that would put her at ease? Can I even help her calm down at all? No, I can't.

"Who...are you...?"

My hands clench into fists. I can't explain anything, so I have to just take her frightened stare. I want to tell Mogi everything right now. She might understand my situation.

But I know it would be the wrong thing to do.

I have to fight. I have to beat the Rejecting Classroom.

In order to do that, I have to reject the daily life it's forcing us to relive.

I set myself on that course the moment I took Otonashi's hand. I'll throw it all away. The idea that Mogi might smile at my words someday, that she might blush, that she'll let me rest my head in her lap—all of it.

With no explanation forthcoming from me, Mogi gives up trying to understand and stands, frightened.

She begins backing away from us, obviously praying that we won't come after her, before turning and running away on feet so unsteady it seems she could topple over at any moment.

I watch her go, never once averting my gaze.

This is exactly the way I hoped things would happen.

"I can tell you're determined."

Otonashi saw everything from where she was leaning against the guardrail.

"That's why I've made up my mind, too. I won't focus my efforts anymore on obtaining the Box in order to achieve my goal."

"…What?"

This is a problem. I can't have this. I need Otonashi.

I'm about to cut in and try to stop her, when…

"Instead, I'm going to help you."

"…Huh?"

Those are the last words I expected to hear from her.

Help me? Aya Otonashi is going to help *me*?

"You're standing there like some sort of slack-jawed idiot. I said I'm going to work with you. Didn't you hear me?"

This goes against the laws of nature, like the sun rising in the west and setting in the east.

"I was lost. As you pointed out, I killed you and, in doing so, reduced myself to something less than human. I just didn't want to admit it, so I became a coward who denied it and fled from her own purpose. The bottom line is that the Rejecting Classroom had me beat. I'm just a Box, and after that defeat, I went astray, believing there was no longer anything I could do."

Though she's berating herself, the strong light burning in Otonashi's eyes fills me with a bit of relief.

"But there's no longer any reason to be lost. I'm ashamed of my actions, but that's no reason to wither in despair. Regrets won't solve anything. I'm through running. I'll embrace my sin and help you as my penance. So please…"

Otonashi closes her mouth, mustering her strength for what she's about to say.

As she begins to speak again, she regards me with something bordering on a glare.

"So please, forgive me."

Ah, now I understand. That's what this is all about.

This strange behavior is her way of apologizing.

However, her entreaty is all but meaningless.

"I can't."

My blunt response seems to catch her off guard momentarily, but she quickly recovers her stern expression.

"I see... It certainly would be impossible to forgive someone for murdering you. That's only natural."

"That's not it."

My words must have puzzled her, because she's frowning.

"I mean...*I don't even know what I'm supposed to forgive.*"

That's right. It isn't that I *won't* forgive her so much as that I *can't* forgive her, because in my mind, she hasn't done anything wrong.

"...What're you saying, Hoshino? I—"

"You killed me?"

"...Yes."

"What're you talking about?"

I can't help but smile.

"I'm right here, aren't I?"

It's the truth, plain and simple.

"I'm right here, Otonashi."

No matter how responsible she feels, it's not like what she did was irredeemable.

In fact, I can't understand why she feels like it was her fault in the first place. It's not like she's the one who made the Rejecting Classroom, after all. She's just caught in its trap like the rest of us.

No, that isn't right.

She isn't just some victim. She's in control. She appreciates how all our minds work and can interpret our behavior. No matter where she throws a stone in here, she knows exactly how the ripples will spread. Otonashi is just as much the master of this realm as the one who created it, perhaps even more so.

It's precisely because Otonashi has so much control here that she feels responsible for everything that happens. She feels that if she only planned better, she could have saved me from death. In her mind, the fact that she couldn't prevent my death, that she didn't prevent it, is the same as having killed me with her own hands.

But Otonashi said it herself: Death in the Rejecting Classroom is a sham.

"It's not weighing on my mind at all. If it still bothers you that much, though, just say what you feel you need to say, and we'll call it even."

Otonashi is motionless, the frown still on her face. When she finally stirs, it's just to lower her head.

"Heh-heh…"

Her shoulders are shaking? Huh? Is something wrong with her? I look her over uneasily.

"Heh-heh… Ha-ha… Ah-ha-ha-ha-ha-ha-ha-ha!"

She's laughing! And *really* laughing, too!!

"H-hey! What's so funny?! I don't get it!!"

My protests seem to fall on deaf ears as Otonashi continues for a moment.

What the hell? …Here I was feeling proud of myself for finally saying something cool, only to find out it all just came across as a joke…

Having had her fill of laughter, Otonashi recovers her usual sternness and addresses me where I stand pouting.

"I have transferred 27,754 times."

"…I'm well aware of that."

"I thought I had a complete understanding of every single thing you could say or do, but I would never have predicted you would say what you did just now. Do you understand how amusing that is for someone as used to boredom as me?"

Otonashi sounds pleased, but it's hard to tell if she's being sincere. I tilt my head, confused.

"You are truly interesting, Hoshino. I've never met anyone like you. You seem so ordinary, with no passion or drive toward anything, but the truth is, there isn't a human being out there as bizarrely obsessed with maintaining the mundanity of normal life as you. That's why you're able to be so clear-cut about the falseness of this world, even more than I am."

More than Otonashi?

"That's not true. I'm not clear-cut about anything. It still hurts to see the accident each time, even though I know soon enough it'll all be like it never happened…"

"Of course it does. That has nothing to do with viewing our situation rationally. When something terrible happens to the characters in books or movies, you feel as bad for them as you would for a real person, right? It's exactly the same thing."

I'm not completely sure, but I think I see what she's getting at.

"Hoshino."

"What?"

"I'm sorry."

It's so sudden that I don't know what she's talking about at first. Her pleasant expression has suddenly vanished.

"The truth is that I was ashamed of my inability to stop what happened. I'm sorry."

"I-it's fine…"

This sincere apology from someone so high above my level is almost unbearable. I stammer over my words like a suspect facing an interrogation. How pathetic.

"I assume that little bit of courtesy takes care of things between us? I will continue to read, understand, and control you just as before. That's what you want, right?"

"Y-yeah…"

"Apologies—I suppose they are necessary sometimes, but I feel like that's the first one I've made in several decades."

I'm pretty sure that's the truth, too.

"Now then, it's almost time."

"Time?"

"Time for the 27,754th transfer to end and the 27,755th to begin."

"Oh, I see."

I'm surprised at how naturally I accept this decidedly odd event as completely normal.

Surveying the area, I see that people have gathered around as they always do when a major accident occurs. I see several of them wearing the school uniform I know so well. Kokone's there, too. Otonashi and I were ignoring all of this, continuing our conversation meant for just the two of us.

Even the normally emotionless Mogi was terrified of Otonashi standing there covered in blood and me talking to her like everything was fine. It's definitely crazy, no two ways about it.

I extend my hand to Otonashi. Someone had rejected that hand once before, but Otonashi quickly reaches out and grips it firmly.

*　　*　　*

My mind is suddenly assaulted by an enormous pressure that threatens to crush it like a vise. The world folds in on itself like a coin purse snapping shut. It's closed, but everything is white. White. White. For some reason I can tell that the unstable surface below us has become something sickly sweet, like candy, as if I can somehow taste it through my skin instead of my tongue. Though the sensation isn't entirely unpleasant, it's still disturbing, and I eventually come to realize that I'm experiencing the end of the 27,754th transfer.

There we are, within the soft, pure-white sweetness of despair.

0th Time

Until I was sixteen, I didn't realize "love changes everything" isn't just a figure of speech.

How many times had I thought that life was too long as I trudged along by force of habit? My fingers and toes probably aren't enough to count the number of times I seriously thought I would be okay with dying.

I was bored. Bored beyond all hope.

I never breathed a word of it to anyone, though, and I kept up the pretense that I was as happy as always. Exposing my true feelings only led to trouble. That's why I did my best to get along with anyone and everyone, regardless of who they were. It's not that hard to do. As long you aren't too picky about your likes and dislikes, what you are and aren't into, you can be friends with anybody.

Everyone flocked to me, and they all said the same thing:

"Oh, you're having so much fun. You must not have a care in the world."

Why yes, you're right. Thank you so much for letting me fool you all so easily. I really appreciate your ever-so-considerate ignorance of all the awful things inside me. Thanks to you, I'm ready to give up everything.

I think I know when this stagnation took hold of me.

Everyone is so selfish.

I told a boy my e-mail address. When I responded to his messages as I normally would, he got all excited and told me he liked me. When I tried to be nice and reached out to a boy who didn't have much luck with girls, he got the wrong idea and confessed his feelings for me. A boy invited me to a movie, and when I went because I found it hard to say no, he professed his love for me. A boy and I happened to share the same path back from school, and after we walked home together several times, he declared his affection for me.

Each one acted so betrayed, selfishly allowed his feelings to be hurt, and started hating me. The girls who liked these boys took it upon themselves to despise me, too—for their own self-centered reasons. The pain stung each time, until one I day noticed I had so many wounds that I could no longer tell which ones were fresh.

I decided not to worry about how I dealt with others and treated them as casual distractions only. I'd maintain a proper sense of the mood and keep my conversations shallow. I'd never show anyone what I was like inside. Like a clam, I'd close my shell tight to protect my tender body.

That was when the boredom started.

No one noticed I was letting them see my outer shell only.

They all kept saying, "Oh, you're having so much fun. You must not have a care in the world."

My efforts were a huge success.

I just wanted everyone to disappear.

It all started one unremarkable day after school. I stood surrounded by strangers pretending to be my friends, and I was making the same frivolous comments as usual with a smile on my face. It was sudden. Nothing prompted it, really.

But the force of it was undeniable. My understanding of my current state took shape in a mere moment, and I was presented with the word that embodied it perfectly:

Loneliness.

Oh. I'm incredibly...lonely.

Solitude. That's what it was. Despite having so many others around me, I felt alone. The term fit so perfectly that I felt a strange sense of comfort in it.

But it wasn't long before that word turned on me with savage fangs. I learned for the first time that unfathomable solitude is inevitably accompanied by pain. My chest hurt, and I found it hard to breathe. Even when I did manage to draw in a breath, my lungs stung as if the air were filled with needles. Everything went black for a moment, and I would've been fine with my life ending right then and there. But my vision soon returned to normal, and my life continued on. I had no idea what I was supposed to do. No clue. *Help me. Help me, everyone.*

"What's the matter?"

Someone realized I wasn't feeling right and called out to me.

"That's quite a smile. You must be having so much fun."

Huh?

I'm smiling...?

Without understanding why, I reached up and touched my cheeks.

They were lifted in a smile.

"I swear you always seem like you're having the greatest time. You don't worry about anything, do you?"

I laughed out loud. "Yeah, I'm having fun," I choked through the spasms. I laughed without even knowing the reason why.

That was when the color began gradually fading from the people around me. One by one, they became transparent. They faded and faded, until I could no longer see them. I could hear voices addressing me from someplace that had nothing to do with me. Then I couldn't make out what they were saying, but somehow I could give a proper response. None of it made any sense.

Before I knew it, the classroom was empty. I was all alone. Somehow, I knew I was the one who had made it that way.

I had rejected them all.

"Well, I've got stuff to do, so I'm taking off."

I couldn't see anyone, but I smiled and said it anyway as I grabbed my bag.

That was how my relationships with others were—my conversations worked whether I was speaking to someone specific or not. I might as well be talking to a wall.

But still, why?

"...Um, are you okay?"

I was sure no one was there, but I heard the words all the same. I had just walked through the school gates, but the voice pulled me back for a moment, allowing me to see the invisible people.

I turned around to find one of the boys from my class gasping for breath. He must have run after me.

I was pretty sure his name was Kazuki Hoshino. We weren't really friends, and nothing about him made much of an impression, so his name was basically all I knew about him.

"What do you mean?"

He would've asked only if he noticed something wrong with me. That meant he'd sensed my shifting attitude, even though nobody near me did.

"Uh…you seemed really…faraway, I guess… I mean, not that I would know, but it's like you're not all there in your life…"

He stumbled over his words. I had absolutely no idea what he was trying to say.

"Anyway…if I've got it wrong, that's okay. Sorry for being weird."

The boy awkwardly started moving away from me.

"…Wait."

He stopped, tilting his head slightly.

"U-um…"

I'd stopped him from leaving, but what was I actually going to say?

Also, how had he been able to describe me as "faraway" as I stood there grinning in that empty classroom?

"……Hey, do I look like I'm always having fun?"

If he answered this like everyone else, that meant he was no different from them.

Oh. I was actually incredibly hopeful. I really, truly wished that he would give me a negative response, that he would understand me.

"Yeah. You, um…seem like you are."

It seemed like he struggled to say that.

The instant I heard his answer, I became disenchanted with Kazuki Hoshino. He was meaningless to me. I hated him. I despised him. I was surprised how rapidly my emotions changed, like a pendulum swinging in the opposite direction, but that exemplified how much I'd hoped he would be different.

But then this boy, who I had instantaneously come to hate, finished speaking:

"You're working hard to appear that way, aren't you?"

Again my emotions swung like a pendulum, this time away from loathing. My change of heart didn't show on my face, but my chest grew strangely warm.

I was working hard. *I was trying so hard to look like I was having fun.*

He was correct. More perfectly correct than if he had simply answered no. That was how I fell in love.

I was well aware that it was just a convenient assumption on my part. Just because he acknowledged my effort didn't meant that he fully understood me. I knew that. But I still couldn't completely dismiss the belief.

At first, I thought my feelings would pass with time, but it wasn't long before I knew there was no going back to the way I was before. My feelings for Kazuki grew and grew, like a pile of snow that never melts, until they engulfed my heart entirely. The possibility that he would soon become my everything weighed on me like a stone, but strangely, I didn't find it unpleasant at all.

Kazuki Hoshino had freed me from my solitary classroom and driven off my ennui.

I knew that if he disappeared from my heart, I would slide right back to where I was before. Right back into the schoolroom of isolation.

The world had changed. It was as simple as that. My previous dull existence seemed like a dream now. My emotions surged as if they were hooked up to a high-powered amplifier. Just exchanging hellos with Kazuki made me happy, but I was sad that it was all we did. Talking to him made me happy, but I was sad we could only chat a little. Something was clearly broken inside me. It was troubling yet pleasant.

Yes! I'll make friends with him no matter what!

My first move is to get on a first-name basis with him.

"Do you have a wish?"

I was in a place that could be anywhere but also nowhere. The figure that addressed me at once resembled everyone and no one. I couldn't tell if they were male or female.

Did I have a wish?

Of course I did.

"This is a Box that can make any wish come true."

I accepted the Box with my blood-soaked hands.

I could tell it was real the moment I touched it. I knew there was no way I could ever give it up.

Who would? There isn't a person on earth who would refuse something like this.

I made my wish.

I knew it wasn't possible, but I made it.

"...I don't want regrets, ever again."

27,755th Time

"Hey, do you notice anything different about me today? Anything at all?" asks Kokone, her features as familiar as ever. I know she's directed this question at me before. What was the answer again?

"...You're wearing mascara."

"Ooh! I knew you'd get it right!"

Looks like I chose the correct response.

"...So what do you think?"

"Yeah. 'Scute."

This smoothly delivered answer also turns out to be correct. My tone wasn't entirely serious, but Kokone grins and nods as if the word "cute" is enough to satisfy her.

"Hmm, I see you've got a lot of promise, Kazu. Maybe that failure of a human being over there could learn a few things from you."

Kokone folds her arms smugly across her chest and turns her head towards Daiya.

"If you're gonna go around saying that, then the quick death of a bitten tongue might be the best option."

"You'd be doing the world a favor, so by all means, go ahead."

"I meant your tongue."

"Ha! Does that mean you're hoping for a deep, passionate kiss? I know I'm adorable, but you've got to get ahold of yourself."

And with that Daiya and Kokone begin their usual rapid-fire

exchange of insults and abuse, completely oblivious to any change in my behavior.

Eventually, Daiya brings up the new transfer student arriving today.

Otonashi can't arrive soon enough.

"I'm Aya Otonashi. I have no use for any of you except Kazuki Hoshino and the owner of a certain item."

The classroom is instantly in an uproar.

Uh, hey, Otonashi? You're a transfer student, so it's easy for you to put some distance between yourself and the class, but I've been a part of this class for almost a year. I can't really do the same.

"What does she mean by 'owner'? Who owns what? Is she talking about someone connected to Hoshino?"

"I think she's just talking about his girlfriend."

"So Hoshino has a girlfriend, and this transfer student Otonashi is looking for her? I wonder why."

"There's probably something going on between him and this Otonashi girl, too! Maybe they're going out...or maybe he's cheating on his girlfriend with her!"

"Yeah, that has to be it! That version is more interesting, so let's go with that!"

"I bet Otonashi got herself tangled up in a messy love-hate relationship with our playboy Hoshino and transferred here in pursuit of him."

"That means Hoshino managed to seduce a hottie like her! Lucky bastard!"

The story spirals onward as everyone ignores that I'm sitting right here. Where the hell are they coming up with this stuff?!

"Actually...Kazu has been stringing me along...," Kokone comments.

"What?! You're the other woman?"

"No...I think I was more of a side fling. I was, like, the third girl in his harem, but I'm pretty sure there were lots of others."

"*Tch*... Damn, what a player!"

Kokone fakes a few tears, and even Daiya contributes to the chaos with a few uncharacteristically loud remarks. It figures they'd choose now to team up, the jerks.

"...What a mess," I hear Otonashi mutter. "I was trying to keep my distance from the class, but now I'm right in the middle thanks to you."

Uh...are you sure it's really my fault?

As soon as first period ends, Otonashi and I make a mad dash from the classroom. Naturally, this sets everyone off, with a few of the boys in particular shooting me dirty looks, but I pay none of it any mind.

We arrive at the usual spot behind the school.

No more class for us.

"I see. Now I know that the trade-off for winning you over to my side is being mired in all your relationships. Damn... What a pain!"

Um, no, the real issue is with how you introduced yourself.

"But this is the first time in 27,755 transfers that giving the class the cold shoulder has become a disadvantage. It's truly interesting."

"Well, you may be having fun with it, but I'm certainly not..."

"Don't be like that. I can get a little excited when I come across something new like this. I never imagined cooperating with you would change things so much. This is a welcome opportunity for us."

"What do you mean?"

"I mean we could come across some new facts I might not have found on my own."

When she puts it that way, working together might make this all worth it. But still...

I have to admit Otonashi is onto something, though. After all, she had no idea what Class 1-6 was like before today. She had no point of comparison. One good example is how she had no clue my feelings for Mogi appeared suddenly between yesterday and today—in other words, during the loops of the Rejecting Classroom.

"But how exactly do we proceed from here?"

"...That's the thing, Kazuki. Perhaps you hold the key to the Rejecting Classroom."

"Huh? So does that mean you still suspect me?"

"Not at all. Let me ask you this: Why do you retain your memories?"

"Uh...I don't know?"

"It's puzzling, right? There's definitely something about you that sets you apart from the other people here, but even then, doesn't it seem strange that you're the only one with memories from before?"

"Well...yeah, of course."

"My theory is that this is also part of the owner's plan."

"Uhhh..."

"You're as slow as ever. Basically, *allowing you to hold on to your memories is one of the end goals of the owner.*"

So me retaining my memories is part of the purpose of the Rejecting Classroom? "That's not possible. I don't always keep them, you know. If it weren't for you, I might have lost them like everyone else."

"That's definitely a wrench in my theory. Still, there's a distinct possibility that the flaw in how the Rejecting Classroom redoes the past is the same as the one allowing your memory retention. If we think of it in the simplest terms, the 'bug in the system' could be that you holding on to your memory is messing up the rewind."

It certainly does seem possible, but it's still all so vague and hard to swallow.

"What would be the point in allowing me to keep my memories?"

"As if I'd know that."

...She says that with derision.

"But I do know what emotion above all others stirs people to action."

"Which one?"

Otonashi fixes me with something akin to a glare as she continues.

"Romantic feelings."

"...Romantic...?"

The look on her face is borderline scary, so I don't process the words straightaway.

I get it now, though. Romantic feelings. Love. Yes.

"That sounds pretty cute coming from you."

She fixes me with a chilly gaze.

"What's cute about it? Love that obsessive is basically the same thing as hate."

"The same thing as hate?" I'm perplexed. "...B-but they're totally different..."

"They're the same... Well, I suppose they are a bit different, actually. This kind of love can be an even more vicious emotion than hate if the person is truly unaware their feelings are tainted. It's absolutely horrifying."

Horrifying...

"That's enough talk about that. Do you have any ideas, Kazuki?"

"You mean of someone who might have feelings for me? There's no way anyone could..."

My voice trails off as something trips my memory.

There is someone.

At least, as long as that phone call asking me to meet up wasn't some sort of prank.

"You've thought of someone, haven't you?"

"..."

"What is it?"

"...Uh, so. Just because someone likes me doesn't automatically make them the culprit, right?"

"Of course not. That wouldn't be enough to conclude they're the owner of the Box. We'd still need to investigate them, though."

"No...well... It's just that this person couldn't be the one responsible for all this."

"What makes you so sure they aren't?"

I know why. It's that I just don't want them to be.

"As long as we're in the Rejecting Classroom, we have an infinite number of opportunities to find them. If there's even the slightest chance they could be the culprit, we have to follow up on it."

"...But that way of doing things hasn't ever succeeded before, right?"

"I must have touched a nerve. Yes, that's right, but the idea that the owner wants you to retain your memory is an entirely new perspective. I've never started my investigations from there. We may be able to glean some information I never could before."

"But—"

"If you really trust them so much, wouldn't you want to clear up any possible doubts about them?"

Of course. She's right.

The truth is that I do have doubts, and I'm afraid of what we might find if we started digging.

"...All right, I understand now. I'll help you."

"You shouldn't be helping. You should be taking the lead."

...She's right about that, too. I'm the one who wanted out of the Rejecting Classroom, after all.

There's something that's bothering me, though. Something feels really off.

"At any rate, let's get to work."

"H-hold on a sec."

"What's there to hesitate about?! I've had about as much of this as I can take!"

What seems so wrong...? Oh yeah. That has to be it.

"What's the matter, Kazuki? Your face is red."

"Uh, well, it's just that..."

Why is she calling me Kazuki instead of Hoshino?

"What? You aren't making any sense. Hey, why are you blushing?"

"...S-sorry, just forget about it."

When did she start calling me by my first name? Not even my parents call me that.

My face must be getting even redder.

"...? You're strange. Anyway, we need to get moving."

Otonashi turns around and walks off.

"O-okay..."

Maybe I should start calling her something besides Otonashi. Maybe call her Aya like she calls me by my first name.

...Whoa, whoa, whoa!! Nope, nope, not a chance, absolutely not!!

Maybe something like "Miss Aya"... No, that's really stilted. Going by her last name puts too much distance between us now that we're working together, too. I need something more easygoing...

"Uh..."

Only one thing comes to mind. It's going to be really hard to say, but I've said the name several times already, so I should be able to get used to it.

"...Maria."

I say it softly, just to test it out, but Otonashi instantly stops and turns around. Her eyes are wide in surprise.

"Ack! S-sorry!!"

Her acute reaction makes me apologize reflexively.

"...Why are you sorry? You caught me off guard, that's all."

"...You're not mad?"

"No need to be. You can call me whatever you want."

"I—I see..."

Otonashi—no, Maria—smiles a bit.

"Still, 'Maria' of all names... Heh-heh."

"Ah, well, if it bothers you..."

"I don't care. You just reminded me of something, though."

"Uh... What?"

For some reason, Maria smiles kindly.

"That you're a funny guy, Kazuki."

I'm snooping.

I've returned to the classroom and am now rummaging through the belongings of the girl who has feelings for me.

I don't like what I'm doing, of course, and I'm really feeling like I've strayed from the straight and narrow this time.

It's PE right now, so Maria made the call that it would be better to dig through the suspect's things and find some clues before confronting her directly.

I agreed, though I couldn't bring myself to say so, which is why I went along with the plan despite my wounded morals.

There's no point unless I do some rummaging, too. Maria's already gone through everyone's things many times before. Judging by our current predicament, she hasn't had much luck with it. That makes sense, though. Maria didn't know any of our classmates before today, so she wouldn't be able to tell if anything was weird or not.

"Phew..."

This girl's textbooks are unexpectedly full of neatly color-coded underlined sections, and her notebooks contain small, rounded letters in a vibrant assortment of colors. There's a doodle of a cat in the left margin, and another picture of a cat in the same place on the next page. The same with the page after that, too... That's when I realize that together, the pictures make a flip-book. As I flip through the pages, a cat flies into space on a rocket made out of cans. I have to chuckle at that, which provokes a glare from Maria.

Our suspect's bag is full of the cute articles anyone would expect a girl to have. Most everything is either pink or white. Her iPod is jam-packed with J-pop. She must have her wallet with her, because it's nowhere to be found.

"Oh!"

I find a cell phone covered with pretty decorations. A treasure trove of personal information.

My hopes of finding a few leads are dashed to bits when it turns out the phone is locked. I won't be able to explore its hidden secrets, but I'm kinda glad I don't have to look through it, too.

Next, I open the makeup pouch beside a pink mirror. This must be foundation, and that's probably some colored lip balm. Here's a pencil for drawing on eyebrows and scissors for trimming them, and this brand new one here must be...mascara.

"..."

Huh?

Something isn't right.

"Did you find something, Kazuki?"

"......I'm not sure, but..."

I dig through the makeup bag. There doesn't seem to anything suspicious inside.

"Maria, what do you think of this pouch?"

"Well, I've certainly seen it before, but I never found anything strange about it..."

Maria's face freezes as her sentence trails off.

"—Wait, that's impossible. She shouldn't have this. If she did, I would've noticed during the 27,755 times before. But...she actually—"

"What is it? Did you think of something?"

"...Did you notice anything else, Kazuki?"

"...Huh? ...Well, it did strike me as unusual for her to have it."

"How could this be?"

Maria has a pained expression on her face.

I resume digging through the bag to see if anything else turns up. Down toward the bottom, my fingers make contact with a texture I know well. I pull the object out.

"Ah—"

Something is coming back to me.

The familiar packaging triggers a memory.

"So maybe if I'd made a move on you differently, you might've gone out with me?"

"Okay, I get it. I'll just keep after you until you finally return my feelings."

No way.

No way.

No way.

I refuse to believe this. This is BS.

It has to be a coincidence, nothing but a random fluke, but it's too out there for my brain to have made it up…

"Maria, what's your favorite food?"

"…What's with you all of a sudden?" Maria frowns at me. "…Hey, what's wrong, Kazuki? You look pale."

"…Mine is Umaibo."

I show Maria what I found in the bag.

It's one of my flavored rice sticks.

"My favorite is corn potage, but I've never told anyone because nobody really cares. I snack on them in class all the time, but I'm always eating different flavors since I like to give them all a try. There's no way anyone would know that I like corn potage the best."

"You aren't such a big fan of the teriyaki burger flavor, though."

"Which one's your favorite?"

I stare at the snacks again, wanting to believe this is some sort of mistake.

Every time I look, they're always the same.

They're corn potage flavor, not teriyaki burger.

The memory they've conjured up is telling me something.

Even if it's a coincidence that she has a corn potage Umaibo in her bag, the images in my mind are declaring irrefutably that she has to be the owner.

"Kazuki."

Maria grips me firmly by the shoulders. Her nails dig into my skin and drag me back into awareness.

"This is the part where I'd like to say 'She has to be the owner. We finally found her,' but I don't think that's the case..."

She sounds so bitter that I have to ask what she means.

"There's no way the person who managed to fool me for 27,755 transfers would make such a careless mistake."

"But I thought you said you never actually knew who the owner was?"

"That's not quite right. For all we know, I could have identified her as the culprit many times before this. But I wasn't able to remember it was her."

"Huh? Why?"

"I'm not exactly sure, but it most likely has to do with the rules of the Rejecting Classroom. It's not impossible when you think about it. The Rejecting Classroom will exist as long as the owner continues to believe time is looping. If they're identified, it would cause the whole premise of the classroom to collapse. That's why the rules are set up so anyone who learns the identity of the owner will forget."

"...But this time we found out it's her."

"True, but it's no cause for celebration."

Maria continues angrily.

"What I mean is that if we don't do something this time, we'll lose everything we've learned."

I can see what she means. If we mess this up, our memories will be wiped, and we'll have to start our hunt all over again from scratch.

Maria is grinding her teeth in vexation. She's used to having as many tries as she needs, so she finds this situation with no room for failure extremely irritating.

"...Hey, you normally only get one try in the game of life, anyway.

There's no pressing the reset button and loading from a save point, not even for the little things."

I thought that sounded pretty cool, but Maria only gives me a chilly look.

"Did you really think that would cheer me up?"

"S-sorry… You just looked so upset that I had to say something."

Maria's mouth softens at my apology.

"Oh, I'm definitely upset, but it's not because we're in a tight spot."

"…So then why?"

"Don't you see? The Rejecting Classroom hasn't ended, even though I've managed to locate the owner several times in the past. You know what that means, right?"

I tilt my head.

I can't tell if Maria's angry at me, the culprit, or herself as she spits out her next words.

"It means the owner has beaten me every single time."

"Kokone."

"Oh, if it isn't Kazuki Hoshino, Mr. Loverboy himself."

Kokone teases me in her usual silly tone of voice.

It's lunch break. The class didn't go easy on Maria and me after we skipped all our morning classes. Maria put an end to it pretty quickly by refusing to utter even a single word in response. But it seems our classmates can't keep their curiosity in check, because now they're staring. Not that I don't understand why.

"Um, hey, Kokone. Actually, I—"

I stop myself midsentence. Her normally cheerful expression has been replaced by a much more serious one, and she's taken hold of my sleeve.

With a quick glance toward Maria, she leads me from the classroom.

"I have something I want to ask you. No dodging the question."

Releasing her grip on me once we're beside the door, Kokone continues.

"What's going on between you and Otonashi?"

"…Why do you ask?" I already know the answer, but I put the question to her anyway. Her only response is to lower her gaze, though. "It's not that easy to explain."

Kokone remains silent, her eyes fixed on the floor.

"But Otonashi isn't the person I like," I add.

Hearing this, she looks up at me with wide eyes.

"So that means…"

Something catches her attention, though, and she doesn't finish. The action doesn't slip by me unnoticed.

She's peering hard into the classroom, as if searching for someone.

Her eyes stop scanning.

They're focused on Kasumi Mogi.

As of March 1, I wasn't yet in love with Mogi, and I haven't interacted with her at all so far during this 27,755th transfer.

"The truth is, Kokone, there's something I need to ask of you. Could you—?"

"No, it's fine. You don't need to say it. I think I understand things pretty clearly now." Kokone smiles and continues. "How about meeting in the kitchen after school? We can talk about everything there, Kazu." At first, I wonder why she chose the kitchen, but then I remember that Kokone is in the home economics club. "I don't think there will be anyone there today."

Kokone looks at me again as I nod okay. Her expression is unreadable.

"Kazuki."

Maria calls me over from where she was watching on the other side of the door. She's probably signaling to me that it's time to leave.

After telling her I would see her later, I start to turn away from Kokone.

"Ah, hold up a second."

I stop short and face her again.

"Hey, I just want to ask you something. You don't have to answer if you don't want to, though…"

"What is it?"

"Who is it that you like?"

I answer without a moment's hesitation.

"Mogi."

As she hears this, Kokone lowers her head to hide her face. But I see her expression before it's completely hidden. There's no way I could miss it.

Kokone is smiling.

School is over for the day.

As soon as Maria and I rushed into the kitchen after hearing a scream, we knew just how badly we had failed in everything.

We missed this opportunity that would never come again.

Just as expected, Kokone Kirino and Kasumi Mogi are inside. No, to be more exact, Kokone Kirino and *something that was once Kasumi Mogi* are in the room.

The kitchen is covered in blood.

The one behind all of this stands gripping a kitchen knife, its blade still dripping wet.

"Kazu."

The look on her face doesn't change once she notices me.

"...Wh-why...?"

I don't understand. Why did she need to do this?

Mogi is watching me, her diminutive figure drenched in blood, with the same blank expression she always wears. This time, however, the unmistakable gleam of reproach is in her eyes. Yeah, of course there is. There's no doubting that I'm the one who caused this situation.

"It hurts it hurts..."

Mogi's been quietly mumbling this whole time as if casting a curse upon me.

I don't want to hear any of it. Suddenly, I want to plug my ears and block it out, but I don't. I lost free control of my actions the moment I saw Mogi's bloodstained body. Her words force their way into my ears.

I fight my hardest to avoid understanding them, but it's no use. The words swell and surge like an avalanche, pouring over me until they engulf my immobile form.

Mogi is speaking to me.

She's condemning me and voicing her hatred.

"It hurts."

27, 755th Time

"It took me long enough, but I've finally realized I don't need you anymore."

The girl tilts her head in confusion, maybe caught off guard by how suddenly I spoke.

"Surely you realized you were getting in the way? Don't you think that was wrong of you? You and I used to be friends."

But we aren't anymore.

I'm sure she probably still considers me a friend. Up until yesterday, we were so close we would talk about our love lives together. But I've changed. I don't think of her that way now. We aren't friends anymore.

This isn't just because I'm different. It's because she can never doubt anything about the new, changed me. Even if I don't speak to her like I once did, she'll never notice.

"Nothing can keep me from changing."

That's the rule that governs this world.

Say I changed in the normal world, and the others didn't. Like how she still thinks of me as a friend. If something about me was different, it would draw attention as something unusual. That would be enough to interfere with my own evolution. It could turn into something like the mess one of my classmates caused by showing up to school with post-summer-break blond hair. And if I were stuck staying the same in circumstances like that, I couldn't do what I wanted.

Which would prevent me from achieving my sole wish, to greet today with no regrets.

That's why I have this helpful little rule.

Yes, this world was made so everything would work in my favor.

★   ★   ★

Even so...

Even so, what? I can't think of anything past that point.

I get the feeling I shouldn't.

That's why I decide to stop trying and choose a different topic.

"Love is a lot like spilling soy sauce on white clothes, don't you think?"

Her head is inclined, as if she doesn't understand my comparison.

"It happens sometimes, right? And even if you wipe it off, it'll always leave a stain. It'll be there forever, so every time you see it, you're going to remember that time you spilled soy sauce on yourself. It'll always be there, so there's no way to forget."

I open a drawer in a cupboard.

"Pretty frustrating, right?"

I grip the knife inside the drawer.

"That such a stain was able to break me."

I pull out the knife.

I've used this implement several times before for this very purpose. It's the sharpest one here.

She goes pale at the sight of what's in my hand.

Even though she probably has a pretty good idea of what comes next, she still asks me why I'm doing this. Maybe a part of her still believes I'm not going to do what she thinks I am.

"What am I doing? Ha-ha."

Sorry, but I think this might...

"I'm rejecting you."

...go exactly the way you feared it would.

I xxxxx the xxxxx into her xxxxxxx.

I try not to process the agonizingly black emotion threating to well up inside me. It's impossible to resist, and all of this would be pointless if not for its presence, but I still fight it anyway. I don't want to experience this feeling. I just want to keep pretending I don't know what it is.

She collapses, and blood spews from her mouth.

She looks like she's suffering. Poor thing.

I've probably messed things up. I should have kxxxed her quickly so she wouldn't have to go through this pain.

"Making a mistake at this point can be pretty scary, you know. Boys get insanely strong when they're in danger. Even the skinny guys are several times stronger than I am. It really hurts if they hit you when they're terrified like that. What's really frightening about it is that look in their eyes. Like I'm trash. How did I mess up last time again...? Oh yeah, I used a thin knife that looked cool. It wasn't really meant for killing people. That's another thing—stabbing and cutting people is very unpleasant. It's gross. I even throw up sometimes. And then I start crying because I don't understand why everything has to be so awful for me. But in the end, as long as the same people keep doing the same things, the results will never change, and the future I wished for will never come. That's why I have to get rid of them. I don't have any other choice. It's horrible. Why have I been forced to do this?"

The girl stares at me, the vitality fading from her eyes.

"The truth is, maybe I didn't need to stab you like this. 'Rejecting' someone all comes down to my prerogative, you know? I haven't found any other effective method besides this, though. I've never been able to do it successfully without killing them with my own two hands. Completely erasing someone from the bottom of my heart is harder than you'd think. It weighs on my mind. I avoid that person out of guilt. Once that happens, I realize I never want to see them again and finally reach a place where I can truly 'reject' them. Once I do that, no one remembers them, not even me, no matter what happens."

Her head is hanging limp, as if she no longer has the strength to look up at me.

"I understand. I'm terrible, right? All of this is awful. But what else am I supposed to do? ...Sorry, it's not like you would know. Ahh, why do I always blabber on like this? I know. I'm scared, so scared that I just can't keep quiet. I want to think that if I explain why I do all this, maybe someday one of you will forgive me. But I understand. There's no way you can forgive me for this, right? I'm sorry. I really am. I'm sorry, I'm sorry. I'm sorry for being so selfish. But I'm the one who is suffering the most, don't you see? I blame myself for all of this. I know I'm a horrible person. So I honestly couldn't care less what you think of me."

Who am I talking to?

I realize it doesn't matter, though. I was never speaking to anyone, ever. I never thought of the person collapsed on the floor here as my friend.

No matter what, I'm always alone.

"N-no—"

I still don't want to admit it, though.

I say all this as I remain in this place that isn't mine, continually being reminded of how alone I am whether I like it or not.

Come on.

Hurry up and get here.

"*Kazu.*"

When did I start calling him that? We became close several times during the endless loops, and he even gave me permission to use his first name, but he'll never remember any of it.

That's when the door opens.

And there he is.

Kazuki Hoshino, the object of my obsession.

He stops short and stands in shock as he beholds the grisly scene before him. Beside Kazuki is that sour-faced, interfering Aya Otonashi, that parasite who lives off the Boxes.

"...You finally came, Kazu."

I'm disgusted at my own words.

How stupid am I?

How many times has Kazuki failed to live up to my expectations? You'd think I would have thrown him away time and again after these countless betrayals.

He isn't here by coincidence. I braced myself, invited him here, and showed him this scene.

Despite this, I always hope for a miracle when Kazuki arrives like this. I hope he'll take me from this place back into the real world.

That'll never happen, though.

Kazuki's eyes are open wide.

"Kazuki, I understand how you must feel, but you knew this was what we would find." That unwanted nuisance is saying something.

"The owner is Kasumi Mogi."

*　　*　　*

Kazuki looks at Xxxxxx Xxxxxx with eyes as round as saucers. Her name? Oh, I forgot it. I can't even remember when it left my memory.

"Wh-why?"

Why did I do this?

I can't hide my anger at Kazuki's failure to understand such a simple thing.

My eyes curse Kazuki as I bare my heart to him.

"It hurts."

Saying it just once doesn't help.

"It hurts, it hurts."

It still isn't enough.

"It hurts it hurts..."

Even so...

"I want to live."

27, 755th Time

Now that I think about it, Mogi isn't wearing any makeup. Unlike Maria, I don't know much about cosmetics, so it doesn't jump out at me at first.

But Mogi has a makeup pouch in her bag.

Why?

Maria's theory is that she got tired of it.

I can't remember at all, but I'm sure at one point Mogi used to care about her appearance. In the Rejecting Classroom, though, she could no longer see the meaning in making herself look good and eventually just stopped trying. The pouch is still in her bag, as it was on March 1 before the Rejecting Classroom came into being. Now Mogi finds putting on makeup and even taking it out of her bag to be a pain.

The only person who would reach such a state would be someone with over twenty thousand transfers' worth of memories, and the only person capable of having those would be the owner.

Which means the owner is Kasumi Mogi, the one I love, and the one who loves me.

"There's something I have to tell you, Kazu."

Kokone said something like that when she asked me to come meet her during the 27,754th loop.

"Kasumi likes you."

She knew how Mogi felt about me. I'm sure she was friends with her *until yesterday* and even offered her advice.

We wanted to call Mogi out, but doing so would put her on guard. With her having outwitted Maria so many times in the past, we couldn't afford to give her any time to prepare.

That's why we decided to involve Kokone and take advantage of her busybody nature. If we could somehow convince Mogi that I was going to confess my love to her, she just might show up.

That resulted in Kokone being murdered.

I remember what Mogi said to me.

"Will you go out with me, then?"

I wonder how many times she's asked me this. How long has she liked me? If the feeling was mutual, then why did she say what she did?

"Wait until tomorrow."

That's how she answered me, right?

Mogi seems oblivious to the blood everywhere, her face blank.

Just like it always is.

Was she so emotionless in the past? I don't think so. There's a bright and smiling Mogi in some of my memories, but she doesn't seem the slightest bit real. The only Mogi I can imagine is this cold and silent one before me.

What if the Mogi that was full of life, the one I've never met, is the real Mogi?

Where did she go?

"She's been consumed." Maria answers my unspoken question. "The endless cycle of repetition has devoured every last bit of her," she says, regarding the emotionless Mogi with contempt.

I'm reminded of something I thought once before, that there's no way the human mind can withstand so much repetition.

Mogi went through all of this 27,755 times, and now here she stands bathed in blood.

"...It's Kazu's fault," she declares, her eyes fixed on me. "Kazu drove me to this!"

"...Mogi, what did I do?"

"*Mogi*," she echoes, the left side of her mouth twitching upward. "I told you. I know I've told you. I've told you hundreds of times."

"Wh-what are you talking about...?"

"I told you to call me Kasumi!!"

...I didn't know that. How could I?

"I told you hundreds of times, and you listened hundreds of times. So why? Why do you always forget?"

"I mean... There's nothing I can do about that..."

"Nothing you can do about it?! What is that supposed to mean?!"

Even though Mogi is screaming hysterically, her face is still almost entirely devoid of emotion.

I'm sure that over the course of the thousands of repetitions, she's lost sight of the meanings behind different expressions and forgotten them entirely. She can no longer laugh, cry, or grow angry.

"Don't listen to her, Kazuki."

Mogi finally turns her glare toward Maria.

"Don't call him that like you know him so well!"

"I'll call Kazuki by whatever name I choose."

"No, you won't! ...Why does he remember you and not me...?"

"Mogi, you're the one who made it this way. This type of system makes it easier for you to do things over."

"Shut up! I never wanted that!"

Now that you mention it, Mogi did seem frightened that I remembered Maria during the 27,754th loop.

At the time, I thought my strange behavior was what set her off, but knowing she's the owner puts a different spin on things. Seeing that I remembered Maria and not her detonated all of Mogi's pent-up frustration and sent her into a panic.

"Kazu..."

I'm not used to having Mogi call me that. No doubt she's asked me if it's okay to call me Kazu, just as she told me to call her Kasumi.

I forgot, but she never did.

"You said you liked me, Kazu."

"…Yeah, I'm sure I did."

"I returned your feelings. I said I liked you, too."

"…"

My only recollection is of Mogi telling me to wait until tomorrow. I can remember nothing else.

"I don't remember you saying that."

I don't have any other answer for her.

"Do you know how happy that made me? I worked so hard every time things started over to make you notice me. I tried changing my hair, putting on mascara, flirting with you, learning your hobbies, learning how you talked… And then you know what happened? A miracle. Something about you clearly changed. I could tell you were interested in me. You were receptive, even though you turned me down so many times before. And would you believe it—you even confessed your feelings to me! My efforts finally paid off. I thought there was something next, something I would enjoy. I even thought this incessant repetition might come to an end. But then… But then, you…"

Mogi stares at me without a hint of emotion.

"You forgot."

I lower my head, unable to hold her gaze.

"You forgot, but I had faith that the next time you might not. Each time I confessed my love to you, each time you confessed yours to me, I had hope, such great hope, but you never, ever remembered. Before too long, I gave up trying to make you remember, but I couldn't stop that faint glimmer of hope each time you said you loved me. Who knows? Miracles do happen, right? But that's also why it hurt more and more every time, more than you could ever imagine."

I was never able to imagine myself in a relationship with Mogi, yet she somehow managed to make this impossible thing into a reality during the endless loops of the Rejecting Classroom. She made me fall in love. Maybe that's why the memories I do retain are always so vague.

But even if she did, it was pointless.

There would never be anything beyond that point.

She would win me over, and then it would end.

This love was doomed to be unrequited.

There would be no relationship, no gold at the end of the rainbow; her feelings would never be reciprocated.

"That's why I eventually stopped wanting you to confess your feelings. But that didn't stop you from saying it. You kept saying you liked me. It made me happy, but it hurt even more. That's why I had no choice but to say what I did."

Mogi repeats that phrase I've heard so many times in the past.

"Wait until tomorrow."

My chest tightens.

Those words brought more suffering to Mogi than they did to me, even though I was on the receiving end of them.

If all this is true, then why didn't she try to put an end to the Rejecting Classroom herself? Her feelings will never be rewarded, and even if that isn't her main objective, it's plain to see she's experiencing unimaginable suffering.

"Kazu...do you understand now? It's your fault that I'm in pain. All of it, everything, every single last bit of it is because of you."

"What a joke." Maria angrily interrupts Mogi's monologue. "You're obviously just trying to pass the buck to someone else. Admit it. You couldn't take the pain of your own Rejecting Classroom, so you want to claim Kazuki is the one responsible."

"...No! It's his fault this hurts so much!"

"You can think that if you want. But I know Kazuki doesn't feel that way. It's not even possible for him to remember you. He only has what memories he does now because he has his own purpose. It has nothing to do with your twisted love."

"That's... How do you know that?!"

"How, you ask?" Maria stands tall, her tone mocking. "The answer is simple."

Her next words are chilly and to the point.

"No one in the world has watched Kazuki Hoshino more than I have."

"Wha—?"

Maria's sharp claim sends Mogi into silence. Her mouth opens and closes as if she's trying to come up with a retort, but no words are forthcoming.

My mouth is shut for an entirely different reason. It's hard not to be embarrassed when someone says something like that about you.

"B-but I've been watching Kazu for just as long—"

"That time was worthless."

Maria's comeback is unfounded, meant to provoke.

"From the way things have turned out here, it's obvious that time meant nothing. Take a look in the mirror. Take a look at your hands. Take a look at what's lying there at your feet."

On Mogi's face are clots of dried blood, now almost black.

In her hands, the knife.

And at her feet, Kokone's lifeless body.

"So go ahead, say whatever you want. Say that you've been watching Kazuki for as long as I have. But just ask yourself if you believe that means anything."

Mogi's head sinks, as if the very core of her being has shattered.

I can't think of a thing to say to her.

"......Heh, heh-heh-heh. You've been watching Kazu more than anyone in the world? Sure, that might be true. Heh-heh-heh. But it doesn't matter. It doesn't matter one bit."

Mogi giggles, her head still hung low.

"Hmph, how pathetic. You've finally gone mad."

"Finally...? Heh-heh... What are you saying?"

Without raising her gaze, Mogi turns the point of the knife toward Maria.

"Do you really think I'm concerned with staying sane anymore?"

Mogi raises her head.

"Let me fill you in on a little secret, Otonashi. The people I kill vanish from this world."

Her face is still as blank as ever.

"That's why it doesn't matter! It doesn't matter how much you've watched Kazu, because you're just going to disappear!!"

Mogi lunges toward Maria with the knife. I shout Maria's name, but all she does is watch Mogi rush at her disinterestedly and without a hint of panic. She deftly grabs the wrist of Mogi's right hand, her knife hand, and twists her arm into submission.

"Ngh..."

It's a completely lopsided struggle, to the point that I'm embarrassed for yelling.

"Sorry about this, but I've been studying martial arts this whole time. Reading a direct approach like yours just now was as easy as taking candy from a baby."

The knife drops from Mogi's hand with a clatter.

Now disarmed, all she can do is look dazedly at her weapon where it lies on the floor.

"...Just like taking candy from a baby, huh...?" Mogi mutters bitterly, her gaze still on the knife. "...Heh-heh." She's still in pain, but she's smiling.

"Is that funny?"

"'Is that funny?' you say? Ah-ha-ha, ha-ha-ha-ha-ha-ha-ha!"

Mogi's mouth opens wide as the laughter bursts forth. The expression on her blood-smeared face is nowhere close to being a smile, however. Though she's laughing, her cheeks hang slack. Where her eyes should be crinkled in amusement, they're now open even wider than before. Maria grimaces in disgust as she watches.

"Of course it is! You compared grabbing my arm with taking sweets from a child! Oh, that is rich, even from you, the great Aya Otonashi! If this isn't your greatest screw-up yet, I don't know what is!"

"I haven't the slightest idea what you find so amusing."

"Oh really? Then let me ask you this: *Could you really steal something from a baby?*"

I still don't understand why Mogi is laughing, but Maria has fallen silent.

"You got me. Yay, good job, congratulations. So now what? What was it you were trying to do again?"

"..."

"I know. I've heard it many times, in fact. You want to put an end to this world of repetitions, right? You want to get ahold of the Box, right? And how do you go about doing all that? Oh yeah! Don't you need to kill me?"

"...That's right."

"I already knew how skilled you were in the martial arts. You yourself have said so many times before. So why are talking like you outwitted me? You made a complete fool of yourself! Did you really think I wouldn't know any of this? I'm so embarrassed for you! It must be humiliating! Hey, you know I go back to the past each time just like you do, right? I know you front to back, too! I dropped my knife. You've got my arm in a lock. So...?"

Mogi's voice grows serious, and she speaks in a low tone.

"What are you going to do with me?"

"..."

Maria doesn't answer.

"Otonashi, the kind the gentle soul. Otonashi, who could never kill me. Otonashi, who could never torture me. Otonashi, who could never even break a bone. Would that pure heart that abhors violence so much even allow her to wrench something from the hand of a little infant? I don't think so. Absolutely not."

Now I see why Maria was defeated so many times in the past.

Once things escalate to the point where violence is the only solution, she's rendered powerless.

And Mogi is well aware of this.

"Think about it. I could've killed you—rejected you—any time I wanted to. Do you understand why I haven't, even though you're nothing but a nuisance to me? Sure, it can be convenient to have you around, like how you always save me from the accident. But that's not it. I realized something the first time you figured out I had the Box, when you couldn't corner me."

Maria clenches her jaw.

"You're not even worth the effort."

I'm reminded of something Daiya said once. The protagonist was at a disadvantage against the transfer student because she had more information to work with.

Thing was, he actually had it wrong.

It's the protagonist—Kasumi Mogi—who has the information, and the transfer student is the one at a disadvantage.

"I'm sick of this pattern." Mogi sounds deliberately bored.

"But things are different this time. Kazuki is here."

"You're right! How about we try letting things take a different course, then?"

Mogi kicks the handle of the knife on the floor.

Slick with blood, it twirls and skids over and comes to rest against my feet.

"Pick it up, Kazu."

The knife?

I look back down at it.

The knife glints red, even more wet with blood than before.

"C'mon, Kazu, don't you love me? If you really do…"

I look up, watch the words form on her lips.

"…then you'll give me the knife so I can kill you."

What the…?

I don't understand. I know the meaning of the individual words, but I don't understand what she's saying to me.

"Are you listening? I said give me the knife so I can kill you."

There it is again. I didn't mishear.

"What're you playing at, Mogi?! I know you're in love with Kazuki! Why would you ask him to do such a thing?!"

"You're right—I do love him. That's exactly why I want him to die. Kazu is the reason why I'm suffering. That's why I want him to disappear from my sight. It's the obvious conclusion," Mogi says, like it's just common sense. "I knew Kazu was coming this time, so why do you think I let you all think you had tricked me into showing up? I had a mission to accomplish. There was something I decided to do… I decided to kill Kazu." She meets my eyes as she spits, "If I kill Kazu, I can reject him. He'll be gone. If that happens, I'm sure I won't suffer anymore. I can stay here forever."

"Mogi, that's nonsense! You— Ungh! Ah—"

Maria suddenly grunts and falls to her knees. She's holding the left side of her body.

"…? Maria?"

Something is sticking out of the left side of her abdomen.

Huh? Was she stabbed?

"Ah—M-Maria!!"

Maria examines the object in her stomach.

Gritting her teeth, she yanks it out with all her strength, grunting slightly in pain. Her eyes full of hatred for Mogi, she tosses the tool aside. I look at the object clattering to the floor. It's a folding pocketknife.

"You really slipped up. All the martial arts training in the world can't help you if you never see the attack coming. If you were a boy, you'd probably be fighting back right now, but that thin blade will do fine for a skinny little thing like you. Sorry, but you can't bulk up here no matter how much you train. That's just the way this world works!"

Maria tries to stand, but it seems the wound is somewhere vital, because she can't. An unending stream of blood flows from where she has her hand pressed to her side.

"I've experienced a lot here, too, so I figured it's better to keep one of these on hand. I always hide this knife on me."

Mogi approaches until she's right before my eyes. She stoops down and picks up the kitchen knife.

"Ahh!"

There she is, not on guard against me at all, leaving herself completely open, and all I can do is let out a pitiful yelp. It's as if I'm paralyzed. I can't move. All I can do is stand there like a post that's been hammered into place. My consciousness threatens to abandon my body, as if my thoughts have skidded to a halt in refusal to accept the impossible scene unfolding in front of me.

"I told you, Aya Otonashi. It doesn't matter, because you'll be gone soon."

Mogi straddles Maria and raises the knife high.

She brings the blade down without the slightest bit of hesitation. Again and again, until she's certain Maria is breathing no more.

Maria never lets out even the slightest gasp of pain the entire time.

"It's too bad. I might have let you live if you were content with being the annoying little shit-circling fly you are, but no, you just had to try and make a move on my Kazu, so this is what you get."

With that final bit of spite, Mogi stands up.

Maria lies motionless.

For a moment, Mogi looks down at the kitchen knife she plunged into Maria's body over and over, and then she casually tosses it over to me.

Instinct draws my eye to the weapon that drank Kokone's blood, and then Maria's.

"Okay, now it's your turn."

I kneel down, trembling in fear, and gingerly reach out to touch it. I can't stop myself from pulling my hand back at the slippery texture. Trying to swallow my terror, I extend my hand once more. It won't stop shaking, and I can't seem to grasp the knife. I close my eyes and somehow manage to pick it up. My eyes open. I'm holding the knife that stabbed both Kokone and Maria, and that fact makes my hands shake even harder. I feel like I'm going to drop it. I grip it with both hands to keep the trembling in check.

It's no good.

There's absolutely no way I'll be able to use this knife to do anything.

"What're you doing, Kazu? Hurry up and give it to me."

No, it isn't just me. *None of us should be able to use this to do anything.*

If so...

"...Who made you do this?"

Not even Mogi should be capable of all this. It just isn't possible...

As long as nobody's manipulating her.

Mogi gives me a puzzled look.

"...What're you talking about? Are you trying to say somebody ordered me to do this? Are you okay, Kazu? You know that isn't true."

"But I fell in love with you."

"Why are you saying that now?"

"The Mogi I know would never do any of this, no matter how desperate she became, not even after twenty thousand times through the cycle. The girl I fell in love with would never do this!"

Mogi seems at a loss for words for a moment, but she soon gives me an angry look and makes her reply.

"Oh, I get it. You're trying to appeal to my emotions so I'll spare you. How despicable. I never knew you were this much of a coward, Kazu. You aren't willing to lay your life down for mine, are you?"

Of course I'm not. I don't want to die, and I don't think doing so would save her.

"...Kazu, do you think it's wrong to kill another person, no matter the reason?"

"...Yes."

"Hee-hee-hee. Oh, how noble of you! Yes, you're so amazingly just. I can hardly stand it."

Mogi stares into my eyes as she speaks.

"Well then, how about spending your whole life...no—*forever*—*inside this endless loop?*"

Her words are cool and heartless.

She must know full well that's the last thing I want.

"After all, *if I give you the Box, I'm going to die.*"

Does she mean she'll die if the Rejecting Classroom comes to an end? Maria never said anything about that.

"Do you understand? Removing me from the Box is the same as killing me. Do you think I'm lying? Do you think I'm just saying whatever it will take to protect the Box? Well, I'm not. If you give it some thought, you'll know I'm right. I mean, why do you think I wanted to return to the past in the first place?"

What would make her want to redo time? Maybe if something happened that couldn't be undone?

"Hey, don't you think it's funny that I'm the one who always gets hit by the truck? Sometimes Aya Otonashi would take my place, but... Oh, wait! You did get hit instead of me a few times! But in general, it's always me."

"Ah!"

No way...

I finally touch upon a plausible reason why Mogi has never tried to put an end to the Rejecting Classroom.

That traffic accident is an unavoidable phenomenon within the world of the classroom. The truck always hits someone, most especially Mogi. For some reason, it's inevitable.

I once said that I didn't believe there was any way to change things that had already taken place. Maria responded that it was normal to feel that way, and that the owner most likely felt that way, too.

So even if I had the opportunity to destroy the Box, the moment I did, it would mean—

"Are you prepared to let that truck kill me?"

—I would end the life of the person I loved.

There's a loud clanging noise. I'm not sure what it is at first, but it's the sound of the knife slipping from my hand.

"You couldn't even give me this yourself. How pathetic…"

Mogi walks up beside me and picks up the kitchen knife.

She's going to kill me.

Having committed so many crimes already, the only way for Mogi to rationalize any of this is to keep committing more. Otherwise, the weight of her conscience would crush her. There's no coming back for her. She's lost all means of restraining herself, and now her rampage is going to kill me. She's even capable of murdering someone she loves.

I'm sure that from the moment she committed her first homicide, Kasumi Mogi was no longer Kasumi Mogi.

Her emotionless mask of a face is spattered with the blood of two people.

I can no longer stand, so she kneels down to my height.

She puts her arms around me, the knife still in her hand.

Her arms rest on my shoulders, and she places the blade against my carotid artery.

Mogi brings her face close to mine, opening her mouth to speak.

"Just keep your eyes closed, if you can."

I do as I'm told.

Something soft touches my lips.

I know instantly what it is.

At long last, I feel a certain emotion boiling up within me, the one I didn't feel when I saw Kokone's lifeless body or even Maria's stabbing: rage.

I can't allow this.

"This isn't the first time we've kissed, you know. Sorry it always has to be forced like this."

I will never forgive her. I don't remember any of those kisses, and I'm sure I won't remember this one.

"Good-bye, Kazu. I loved you."

Is she really satisfied with just a bunch of made-up memories she can never share? It's entirely possible. She's become that used to solitude.

I feel a sharp pain run along the muscles of my neck.

I open my eyes in defiance of Mogi's request to keep them closed.

She seems flustered under my silent reproach, but the suddenness of it all means she never takes her eyes off me. Yes, I'm finally able to meet her gaze directly.

I grab Mogi's hand.

From the corner of my vision, I can see a red liquid flowing from my neck and dripping from her hand.

"...What do you think you're doing?"

"I...can't allow this."

"What, are you trying to say you'll never forgive me? Heh-heh... That's fine. I already knew that. But it doesn't matter. This is good-bye, after all."

"You're wrong."

"...About what?"

"It's not you who I can't forgive—it's the Rejecting Classroom that's stolen away our normal lives!"

I tighten my grip on Mogi's slender wrist, completely restraining her arm.

My vision goes black for a second. Maybe the bleeding from my neck is fatal.

"L-let go of me...!"

"No!"

I still don't know what to do. I know I won't be able to kill Mogi. Even so, the knowledge that I can't allow the Rejecting Classroom to go on burns bright and clear within me. That's why I can't let myself disappear here.

"Let me kill you! Please, let me do it!"

Mogi is screaming. Her words are meant to push me away forever, but they only sound like cries of pain to me. Like she's wailing in agony.

...Yeah, I see it now. It took me a long time, but I've finally figured it out.

Mogi is crying.

On the outside, she's as blank and emotionless as ever. There are no tears running down her cheeks. I look at her directly. She instantly averts her eyes. Her legs, so slender that it's almost a surprise they can support her own weight, are trembling. With her facial expressions gone, Mogi can no longer recognize her own feelings. She doesn't even know when she's crying. She has no more tears. I'm sure they all dried up long, long ago.

I'm sorry I didn't notice sooner, Mogi.

"I won't let you kill me! I won't let you reject me!"

"Shut up! Don't make me suffer any more!"

I'm sorry, but begging won't work on me.

That's why I yell, "I'll never leave you in this place by yourself!"

I think I feel Mogi's strength waver for a moment.

But then...

"Ah—"

Everything goes pitch-black. A slap to my cheekbone temporarily restores my vision, and the scene looks different than it did before. Mogi's red-black slippers are directly before my eyes. My hand is no longer holding her wrist and instead lies limp on the floor.

Mogi didn't do anything to me. I just collapsed on my own.

I had just reached a point where I could possibly get through to her, and now my body won't work. I can't even move my mouth properly.

"I'm so stupid."

I can hear Mogi's voice.

"With just a few words, a few simple words, I..."

Unable to lift my head, I can't see what Mogi's face looks like.

"......I have to...kill. I have to kill. I have to kill. I have to kill. I have to kill. I have to kill. I have to kill. I have to kill. I have to kill. I have to kill. I have to kill."

Mogi is repeating the same phrase over and over, as if trying to convince herself.

Her slippers move. Someone's blood splashes, a few drops spraying my face.

I can faintly see the gleam of the kitchen knife.

Yeah, she's going to use it on me.

"This time it's really good-bye, Kazu."

Mogi kneels down and gently strokes my back.

"I have to kill."

She then plunges the blade into...

"I have to kill myself."

...her own body.

27,755*th* Time

"I have to kill myself."

I repeat this mantra to myself frantically. I have no other choice. It's the only way to keep the false "me" from taking control again.

I give up on everything.

I can't think of any other way to atone for the things I've done.

There's a knife stuck in my body.

I'm lying on top of Kazu where he's sprawled on the ground. His face is so close. Eyes wide, he finally notices what I've done.

Don't look at me like that. I try to smile and put him at ease, but I realize I no longer can. It's been so long since I smiled or cried.

The warmth bleeds from my body. Everything inside me is draining out. I hope the despicable things inside me will all be purged, too.

"I'll never leave you in this place by yourself!"

Thank you, but I know that isn't possible. It was never possible from the very beginning.

You knew that, right? After all...

...I've been dead this whole time.

0*th* Time

Ah. I'm about to die.

Time seems to drag on interminably as I lie where I landed after the truck sent me flying. There's no surviving an impact like that. I'm going to die. This is the end.

N-no...

I've wished I was dead plenty of times before, but those were foolish thoughts from someone who never seriously considered what dying really means.

Death. The end. Nothing more after this point. I'm learning how terrifying all of this is in my final moments.

If this is what dying is, then I wish I could have died before love changed my world.

But I know love now...

I have a purpose...

I haven't even been able to reach out to the one these feelings are for...

It's all too horrible.

"Hmm, well, isn't this an interesting situation."

A man (or maybe a woman?) suddenly appears. I have no idea how they got here. Why are they able to speak to me like this is normal? It's unclear where they are in relation to me. I turn around and around, but I can't even tell what direction I'm facing. All the same, I know their eyes never leave me. None of this is possible. No, that isn't true. This is some other place. The strange person is right in front of me, but I can't figure out where that is. This place is perfectly nondescript, yet special.

"No, I'm not talking about your accident. That kind of thing happens all over the world. What interests me is the fact that the accident took place next to a certain boy who caught my eye."

What is this person talking about?

I've heard of people seeing apparitions before they die, but never anyone being transported to some strange place to have a conversation like this.

I wonder if this person is a spirit of death or something.

The figure before me looks like no one, but at the same, I feel like they could become anyone.

There's one thing I'm certain of, however: This person is wonderful.

Silhouette, voice, scent—I find everything about this mysterious figure enchanting.

"I'm curious about something. How will he react to a Box used near him? Oh, and I am rather intrigued to see how you would use one, too. All humans interest me, you see, even if just in passing."

None of this makes any sense to me, but I can see the person smile.

"Do you have a wish?"

A wish?

Of course I do.

"This is a Box that can make any wish come true."

I accept the item.

I can tell it's real the moment I touch it. I know there's no way I could ever give it up.

Please, even if my fate can't be changed, please at least allow me to go back and redo a few things. Even just the previous day is fine. There's still something I need to do. If I can do that day over again, I know I can tell him how I feel. And if I do that, I know I won't have any regrets, no matter the outcome. Please, just give me back a little bit of time. I know it's impossible to undo what's already happened, but that's still what I want.

Once I've voiced my wish, the Box opens its lid like the mouth of some carnivorous beast before fading from sight into the surrounding space.

Yes, okay. That should be fine.

"Heh-heh..."

The person with the charming laugh gives a brief opinion of my wish before vanishing.

"Why do they always hold back...?"

And with that, I'm ejected from that wholly unmemorable yet fantastic place.

I arrive in a dark, damp chamber that reeks with the odor of countless corpses left to rot. The uncomfortable room makes even a jail cell seem like heaven. I'm sure I'll collapse if I spend even an hour here. Soon enough, though, everything becomes a bright white, as if the room is being painted over. The color is so pure, I can't see the boundaries of the room anymore. A scent like incense made from sugar candy drives out the foul smell. With each blink, the space gains a blackboard, desks, chairs, and other classroom fixtures. Once everything is in place, all that's left to do is summon the necessary people, the ones who were in the classroom the day before. Once they're here, we can do it all over. I can redo yesterday.

But no matter how much everything is plastered over, this will still be that chamber worse than a prison cell.

This is my afterlife, packed full of white, white, sweet hope.

That's why I have to do it. If there's no chance of accomplishing my heart's desire, then before all these pretty decorations are stripped away, before my disgraceful actions come to light, I have to destroy this Box with my own hands.

5,000th Time

"Why not just kill them?"

When I ask Haruaki for advice, he jokingly answers with an outlandishly stupid idea.

6,000th Time

"Why not just kill them?"

When I ask Haruaki for advice, he jokingly answers with the same breakthrough he's given me I don't know how many times.

7,000th Time

"Why not just kill them?"

Haruaki jokingly answers with a perfectly reasonable theory.

8,000th Time

"Why not just kill them?"

Haruaki jokingly answers as if to reiterate his logic.

9,000th Time

"Why not just kill them?"

Haruaki jokingly answers me with truth in my most desperate hour.

9,999th Time

He's already told me himself the method I'll use to get rid of him.

"You're looking for a way to make sure that you and a certain person never run into each other again?"

Haruaki has presented many ideas. I listen to them until my ears are numb. In the end, we reach the conclusion we always do: The best way is to make one of the people involved feel shame toward the other person. And then, also as always, Haruaki suggests a way to create a sense of guilt.

"Why not just kill them?"

My back is against the wall, and Haruaki jokingly answers with a final recourse.

"As a last resort. But, I mean, if you kill them, it won't be a question of bumping into them or not anymore!"

Why do I have to reject Haruaki? Because I feel getting rid of him will have the greatest effect on Kazu and me.

Living in that world is like playing an endless game of *Tetris*. At first, I worked hard to get as many points as I could. And it was fun, too. But after a while, I stopped caring. It's just a game in the end, so whether I get a lot of points or not, everything is going to be reset at some point, and I'll have to start from the beginning. Nothing ever changes, even if I get a game over. I still try to find ways to have fun, but even that approach has its limits. It gets boring. It gets tedious. It gets obnoxious. It gets painful. I don't even feel like rotating the blocks anymore. It doesn't matter. It truly doesn't, but no matter how many times I reach my limit, I can't stop. If I do, I'll die. I can't let that happen. I have to accomplish what I set out to do. I have to meet today with no regrets. That's why I have to change the systems and try something else.

Haruaki is one such important part of the structure.

"......Hey, can you tell me how to create guilt again?"

"...C'mon, Kasumi, what's wrong with you? I don't mind, but still..."

Haruaki says it like he always does.

"Why not just kill them?"

This is the thousandth time he's given this answer.

He's right. This is the only choice. Mm-hmm, there's nothing that can be done. *You'll understand, right? But then again, it's a little late for that now.*

—You want me to kill you, right?

10,000th Time

"Stop! Please don't kill me!"

I don't plug my ears.

I'm going to kill Haruaki Usui.

He's the one who suggested it, after all.

I kxxx Haruaki Usui.

That's when I disappear. The me who was once Kasumi Mogi is gone. I have no hope of finding the version of myself that was ground to dust by the agony of this place and scattered to the wind. My body keeps reviving, regardless. It always comes back, even though there's nothing left of me inside.

I feel something entering the empty space within me. Something vile born from this Box. Something grotesque beyond belief with a putrid smell like that of countless dead bugs covered in feces. I try to keep it out. I try again and again. But I know that even if I do, this thing will still worm its way in through the holes in my defenses. It'll tear at my weaknesses like a hyena, devouring those portions and dyeing me pitch-black. Once they're finished with me, I'll no longer know who I am. I'll become a doppelgänger.

But not even that is enough to make me put an end to the Rejecting Classroom.

I still need to greet today with no regrets.

A today where I have no regrets?

"Ah-ha-ha…"

What a fool I am. There's no such thing. This is my afterlife. No matter what I do here, it'll never be enough to sever the ties binding me to the real world. Even Kazu professing his love to me will be meaningless. What can I do to satisfy myself in a world that's completely disconnected, a world with no links to anywhere else? I can't think of any ideas.

The outcome I desired…

I struggled on for so, so long in search of this outcome within the over-riding stagnation of this world.

But the truth is I didn't even know what I was looking for.

I fumbled along in ignorance for some time before eventually reaching the conclusion that the outcome I sought didn't exist.

"I want to live."

Oh, is that it? I finally understand.

So that was my wish.

That also explains why my wish will remain just that—an unfulfilled desire—for all eternity.

My inability to understand all of this warped the Box.

This distorted wish transformed into an obsession that couldn't be dispelled. It will always be here as long as I'm in the Box.

So the fixation remains, spurring the false me into unceasing action. That's how I know that, even if I were to vanish, the Box will never, ever end.

27,755th Time

"I'll never leave you in this place by yourself!"

Kazu's words were enough to momentarily bring back the Kasumi Mogi that had been lost.

"I'm so stupid."

I once made a decision. When all of this started, I told myself that if I lost sight of my purpose, I had to destroy the Box with my own hands before my shameful actions came to light.

But the sheer, overwhelming number of loops in this ceaseless world wore my determination down, diluting it to the point of nonexistence.

All hope of me ever returning should have faded back when I murdered someone whose name I can no longer even recall.

But then...

"With just a few words, a few simple words, I..."

...I was brought back.

My love saved me at the very, very end.

But I know that while I've returned for this moment, I'll lose control again soon.

The Box will consume me, both in mind and body.

That's why I have to kill myself...while I'm still Kasumi Mogi.

"Good-bye, Kazu."

And that's how my Box, which couldn't bring me happiness—even though it could have been so easy—comes to an end.

I die lying atop the one I love. This could be a blessing in itself. I'm okay with this. Yes, this is perfectly fine.

I close my eyes, sure that they'll stay closed forever...

"No one said you could die, you know."

Surprised, I open them again.

Before me stands the mysterious being that gave me the Box. Kazu's eyes must be locked on me, because he doesn't seem aware of the presence.

A calm smile greets me as I meet the figure's gaze.

"I'm not through observing that boy there. I can't have you putting an end to this wonderful opportunity for unlimited study I've worked so hard to arrange."

What? ...What are they talking about?

"Hmm, it might not be enough if we keep to the same routine we have been, though... This goes against my principles, but I'm going to need to borrow that Box of yours for a second. A few adjustments are necessary. You were trying to break it anyway, so you don't mind, do you?"

Without waiting for a response, the being places a hand upon my chest.

"Agh! Aaaaah!!! Aaaaaaaaah!!!"

I'm instantly filled with agony beyond anything I could imagine. The pain is unbearable, even though I've gotten used to being hit by trucks and didn't even cry out when I stabbed myself in the chest with a knife. This sensation is an entirely different variety. It's like having my very soul cut to shreds. It's the sort of pain nothing can alleviate, as if it's being applied directly to my nerves.

The being smiles as they pull the palm-sized Box from my chest.

"You most likely already know this, but this Box won't work without you anymore. I'm going to have to put you inside it."

With those words out of the way, the being begins to fold me up.

I'm doubled over, doubled again, and then put inside the Box.

Kazu. Please, Kazu.

I know what I'm asking is selfish. I know it's laughable to think I have the right to ask anything of you after all I've done. But...I can't... I can't take it anymore...

Help me, Kazu...

27,756th Time

I have to put an end to the Rejecting Classroom and return all our lives to normal.

What's the hardest part of achieving this goal?

Encountering a crazy obstacle, perhaps? Like having to tightrope between two buildings using a piece of kite string? Or repeating the same day a hundred thousand times?

Maybe not. All of those are hurdles I can figure out how to clear. No matter how impossible they may seem, with an infinite amount of time on my hands, I could feasibly acquire the skills needed to overcome them.

No, the hardest part is being unable to tell what I'm up against. If I don't even know where to start, then I'm just stuck. What's more, time doesn't pass within the confines of the Rejecting Classroom. No matter what kind of a jam I'm in, I'll never be able to rely on time to solve the problem.

I'm facing the most difficult of situations right now.

"What's the matter, Hosshi? You seem a bit off today."

It's our first period break. *Haruaki has an easy smile as he speaks to me.*

Class has only just ended, so everyone is still in the room. *Mogi is in her seat. All thirty-eight of my classmates are here.*

I rack my mind for reasons why everyone who was rejected is here again, only to find I have almost no recollection of the previous transfer. I get the feeling I made an important discovery, but for the life of me, I can't remember anything.

That's fine. I can handle that.

If I did find out something of immense importance last time, I can always do it again.

I'm a bit mystified by the return of my classmates, but that doesn't change what I have to do.

That isn't the problem at all.

"Ugh, I'm so bored today… Nothing ever changes."

Nothing ever changes.

Kokone's words spark a dull pain in my chest.

I don't want to believe it. I can't accept the situation before me.

"Hey, Daiya."

As if issuing a plea for help, I call out to my friend.

He remains sitting, turning only his head to look at me.

"Have you heard anything about a transfer student arriving today?"

Despite my faint hope that he would nod, my question is unfortunately met with the exact frown and retort I expect.

"Huh? What the hell are you talking about?"

I knew it. Aya Otonashi will no longer "transfer."

I'm totally on my own now.

Sure, I can find the owner of the Box, but what am I supposed to do after that? Take the Box from them? Destroy it? How am I supposed to go about doing either of those things?

Before, I thought I was working alongside Maria to solve this mystery, but that was nothing more than my pride talking. The truth is that I was totally reliant on Maria, and without her here, I have no clue what to do.

"What I'm saying is that it doesn't matter whether this is normal life or the inside of the Rejecting Classroom. You get me?"

That's Haruaki's counsel.

I was completely stumped earlier, so during break I asked him to hear me out. After telling him everything over lunch, I'm listening to his response as we stand behind the school.

I know Haruaki. He isn't saying this because he doesn't believe my ludicrous story.

"What do you mean, it doesn't matter...?"

"Uh, hey, I'm not saying I don't believe you, okay? But let's just say we are inside this 'Rejecting Classroom' right now. How is this any different from the normal life you want?"

"What do you mean? Everything about it is different."

"C'mon, it's the same. You said all of us disappeared, and now we're back. That Aya Otonashi girl you mentioned was never a member of our class to begin with. Things just went back to normal. You see that, right?"

Things just went back to normal?

...Maybe he's onto something.

I would never have met Maria if it weren't for the Rejecting Classroom.

No one here knows anything about her. And that's as it should be. Aya Otonashi has always been a foreign presence in classroom 1-6.

Maybe everything I'm talking about is just something I dreamed up. Maybe Aya Otonashi is a figment of my imagination.

...I can't tell. But I do know today is still March 2.

"If we're inside the Rejecting Classroom, then it will always be March second. Can you really argue that isn't unusual?"

I thought Haruaki would agree with me, but I was wrong.

He tilts his head a bit to the side as he replies.

"I think you know the answer to that question yourself."

The way he acts like it's so obvious brings me up short. He scratches his head in puzzlement as he watches me.

"I know what you're trying to say, Hosshi. But you only feel that something is wrong because you're aware things are looping. So you've got your everyday average life that you took for granted up until now. If the same day of that life were to repeat over and over, you wouldn't know it, right? I don't feel anything is off right now, for instance. Here, at this very moment, I believe I'm in the middle of the same old boring day-to-day I've always known, even if it does happen to be inside the Rejecting Classroom."

He's definitely right.

The only reason my gut tells me all this is wrong, that it's horrible, is because I know about the classroom. If I didn't, I probably wouldn't notice anything strange at all.

My awareness of the Rejecting Classroom is the source of my mental turmoil. Without that, I could fully enjoy the normal life laid out for me here, even if it's stuck on repeat permanently. The days would roll by as I avoid the sad fate of someone I can't identify. It would all be so happy and convenient.

The idea of destroying all this is nothing more than self-satisfaction.

"It looks like you understand now, Hosshi. So what're you going to do?"

"Right. I know what to do now."

"See? Well then, maybe..."

Haruaki trails off. Wondering why, I turn around and find Mogi standing behind me.

"What's the matter?" I ask.

"Can I borrow *Kazuki* for a second?"

I look at Haruaki for a moment upon hearing her words.

"Anyway, Hosshi, I guess that's probably enough about that for now, huh? Feel free to hit me up if you ever want to talk about it some more."

"Sure. Thanks, Haruaki."

With a quick "You're welcome," Haruaki leaves.

What does Mogi want? Was she looking for me specifically?

I give her face a closer look. I can't help but think how pretty it is, and I quickly look away.

"..."

Her brows are furrowed, even though she's the one who wanted to see me.

"...I'm going to ask you something, and I want you to answer, no matter how crazy it may sound."

"Uh, sure..."

I give my assent, but Mogi's face still tightens as if she finds this a difficult topic to broach. She takes a moment to gather her nerves and then looks me straight in the eyes as she asks her question.

"Am I Kasumi Mogi?"

What?

The question is so out of the blue I can't even act surprised, and instead I stand there without much expression at all.

She averts her gaze in apparent embarrassment.

"......Um, do you have amnesia or something, Mogi?"

"...I know what you want to say, but please just answer the question."

"You're Kasumi Mogi. That's obvious..."

Now that's a line you'd never hear from me normally.

"I see...," she murmurs, seeming slightly sad for some reason. "You might not believe what you're about to hear, but please hear me out. The truth is..."

The next words from Mogi, the Kasumi Mogi who I was in love with, are unbelievably absurd.

"I'm Aya Otonashi."

"...Huh? Aya Otonashi...? You're Maria? But how?"

Mogi continues as I stand there in shock.

"Yes, I'm Aya Otonashi. You and all the others have fallen for this charade where I'm somehow Kasumi Mogi even though I look and talk completely different from her. I have no way to confirm it, but I know for a fact I am Aya Otonashi."

Despite all that she's saying, the only person I see before me is Kasumi Mogi. Still, I can't deny that she does look and speak exactly like the Aya Otonashi in my memory...

"Uh, well, how about this? Lots of manga have stories about people with multiple personalities, right? Maybe you're experiencing something like that right now?"

It sounds ridiculous, but it's still within the realm of rational thought.

"I already considered that. If that were the case, it would be strange that you didn't harbor any doubts about the sudden changes in my personality, and the name Aya Otonashi would never have come up. Don't you agree?"

There's no denying that I never said the name Aya Otonashi to Mogi.

"So why would you have turned into Mogi in the first place?"

"...The way you're describing the situation is misleading. I have only been placed in the role of Kasumi Mogi. I haven't actually transformed into her in the physical sense. I'm happy about that, at least... But anyway, I'll explain how I see this situation. If I'm Aya Otonashi, that means Kasumi Mogi does not exist in the 27,756th transfer. Do you understand?"

I nod.

"Kasumi Mogi is gone. Her position is vacant. I told you before that it was not by my own intent that I was treated as a transfer student in this world, right? This time, I think I've been assigned this empty space instead of being brought in as a transfer student."

It sounds like a bit of a stretch. "But there's no way I, or anyone else in the class for that matter, would mistake you for Mogi."

"That was definitely one of the biggest problems. But when I ran up against this issue, it actually cleared up something else. The owner of the Rejecting Classroom experienced 27,755 of its loops. Their personality should have changed a least once somewhere in all that time, but no one ever noticed anything like that occurring."

I have to admit she might be right.

"It's natural to deduce that some rule of the Rejecting Classroom prevents others from noticing changes to the owner and also prevents those changes from interfering with their personal relationships. Kasumi Mogi was the owner, but for some unknown reason, she has vanished, and now I have taken her place. The aforementioned rule came into effect, so now no one notices anything different, even though my appearance and personality are that of Aya Otonashi."

Her explanation does seem feasible, at least.

If Mogi really is Maria, then I definitely have cause to rejoice. Of course I do. I mean, I would have no idea of what action to take in all of this without her. Maria would be my guiding light.

Still...

"I don't believe you."

I'm just finding it all too hard to swallow.

Perhaps startled by my unexpectedly strong response, Mogi eyes me with a guarded expression.

"I know it's hard to believe, but there's no reason for you to react like that."

I chew on my lip.

"Oh, I see now. You don't want to accept what I'm telling you as true because doing so would be the same as admitting that Mogi was the owner of the Box. You want to avoid that if possible. I can understand why. After all, you loved—"

"That's enough!!" I yell without meaning to.

She's right. There's no way in hell I want to accept any of what she is saying. But it isn't Mogi being the owner that bothers me. No, the thing I absolutely will not accept is...

".......I'm in love with Mogi."

I force myself to say it.

"I know."

Mogi herself scowls as if asking why I'm saying something like that now.

"That's why there is no way you could be Maria!"

My hands clench into fists. Seeing the way they tremble, I'm sure she finally understands what I'm trying to say. Her eyes open wide, and her mouth closes.

I love Mogi.

That feeling will never change, *not even if she looks exactly like Aya Otonashi.*

Let's say everything Mogi is telling me here now is true. That would make me the biggest idiot in the world. It would mean I didn't notice anything different about the girl I loved, despite how much she had changed. I didn't notice even though Maria replaced her entirely. It has less to do with her and more that I can't handle my emotions.

People often say that love is blind, but this would be on a whole other level.

It would all be fake.

It would mean that this love that I've embraced for such an unbelievably long time is false, nothing more than a sham.

That's why I can't accept any of Mogi's arguments. I can't accept the idea that she's Aya Otonashi. The moment I do, this love will die.

"I love you, Mogi!"

That's why I shout those words like a declaration of war.

She falls silent and closes her eyes.

If there's a worse way of telling someone how you feel, I'd like to see it. I'm just crying out my denial of this situation without giving any thought toward her feelings.

I clench my fists even tighter. I've come this far. I have no choice but to say the rest.

"If you really are Maria, then prove it!"

Her eyes remain shut for a short while.

Having steeled her will, she opens them and speaks.

"Have it your way."

I flinch at the strength in her voice.

"You may have succumbed to the Rejecting Classroom, Kazuki, but that doesn't change what I have to do. That's why I thought maybe I would just leave you be. I've decided not to, though. I don't want something like this to bring you to your knees."

As she grabs my right hand, my eyes reflexively go to hers. She never looks away once.

"I want you to know this: I am, and could never be anybody but, Aya Otonashi."

She draws my hand toward her chest.

"Wh-what are you doing?"

"I am a Box." There's disgust in her voice. "That means I'm not a human like Kasumi Mogi."

"Doesn't that just mean you're granting a wish, then? Mogi is like that, too. Even if you could somehow show me the Box, that wouldn't be proof that you're Aya Otonashi."

She shakes her head.

"You've heard stories about fairies who grant a single wish, no matter what it is, right? Did you ever think that for your wish, you would just ask to have more wishes?"

I nod.

Now that she mentions it, I have considered getting infinite wishes that way.

"I'm embarrassed to say that my wish was something similar to that."

Her tone is full of self-mockery.

"I asked to be able to grant other people's wishes. Making others' desires come true is my entire existence now."

"That means..."

She is exactly like a Box.

Still, I thought her wish was a noble one. Why, then, is her smile so self-deprecating?

"Unfortunately, I didn't have complete faith in my ability to do such a thing. The Box didn't grant my wish in its entirety. Everyone who used my powers vanished because *the Box drew upon my feelings that wishes don't come true so easily in the real world.*"

I'm at a loss for words. It's as if these magical objects never grow tired of toying with people.

"Kazuki, I will let you touch my Box. After that, I never want to hear any more nonsense from you about me being someone other than who I really am."

She opens my hand and presses my palm against her chest.

I can feel the beating of her heart.

And then...

"Ah!"

...I'm at the bottom of the ocean. Even on the seabed, it's still bright, like the sun has sunk down here along with me. It's beautiful. I find myself mesmerized by the water. But it's also cold, and I can't breathe.

Everyone looks so happy. So joyful. So jubilant. Everyone is smiling down here under the sea, where they can frolic with the deep-sea fish, where they can drown and bloat and freeze and collapse under the pressure. There's no meaning down here. Nothing overlaps. Each of them has their own puppet show or game of pretend or picture presentation or comedy down here. Everyone is a blissful tragedy.

And in the midst of all this, someone is crying.

Amid all the happy people laughing *ha-ha-ha-ha-ha-ha-ha-ha*, there's one single person who is crying.

I shake my head. This must be some sort of vision. Just a vision. I'm not actually seeing any of this.

But it's enough to make me understand. Someone's emotion, a feeling of hopeless solitude, has been irrevocably embedded in my body.

I surface from the depths of the ocean and return to where I was.

She lets go of my hand.

I slowly pull it back from her chest and sink weakly to my knees.

As soon as my legs touch the ground, I can feel the tears streaming down my cheeks.

It's no use. There's no way I can deny her claims after seeing what I just saw.

"That is the misbegotten happiness of my Box."

She is Aya Otonashi.

But doesn't Mogi have a Box, too? That doesn't matter. It wouldn't be enough to refute Maria's claims. I don't need logic to understand this. A single touch was enough to make me understand that the girl standing before me is Maria.

I'm sure what I saw was something she normally avoided showing to others. She did it for me, though.

All so I wouldn't lose myself to the Rejecting Classroom.

"Maria, I'm sorry…"

Maria smiles and shakes her head.

"…"

I hate my emotions right now.

Even though I understand, deep down in my bones, that she's Aya Otonashi, I can't change my feelings toward her. Her smile is irresistibly cute. The last vestiges of my affection are toying with me, refusing to fade.

My tears keep flowing as I kneel there, disappointed at my inability to completely free myself of this love.

"Kazuki."

Maria says my name.

"Huh?"

Then she does the last thing in the world I would have expected her to do.

She takes me into her arms.

I comprehend the physical action itself but not the meaning behind it.

The hesitant way Maria moves her arms is totally unlike her.

"You're the only one who remembered my name."

I can't quite figure out why she's saying this.

"If it weren't for you, I would've been alone. It pains me to say it, but you just being there supported me in its own way, even when I mistook you for the owner. That's why…"

I finally get what Maria is doing.

"…I'm here to support you now."

Maria is embracing me. Contrary to her words, what she's doing isn't supporting me so much as enfolding me, weakly and timidly.

"I can be kind to you while you're in love with me."

I'm confused.

I can't determine whether the feelings inside me at the moment are for Kasumi Mogi, Aya Otonashi, or both of them.

I do know one thing for sure. Being here like this, right now, makes me the happiest man on earth.

"Ah."

What if…

What if Maria had another reason for allowing me to touch her Box besides just convincing me? She didn't want me to say she was Kasumi Mogi. She wanted me to acknowledge her existence. The notion runs through my head, but eventually, a laugh rises to my lips as I realize how ridiculous it all sounds.

"So what did you and Kasumi talk about, Hosshi?"

A huge grin on his face, Haruaki gives me a little poke in the chest as he approaches me after school.

"Did she have a confession for you, perhaps?"

"Yeah… Uh, I mean, no…"

She did confess she was actually Aya Otonashi, so he's right, in a way.

"You're being evasive! I don't buy it! Wait, don't tell me you're serious?! You lucky bastard! Kasumi's even cuter than usual these days, too!"

Oh, right.

Seeing Haruaki having such a good time with this, I realize what I have to do.

Finding Maria again is reassuring, but now that Kasumi Mogi, the actual owner of the Box, has disappeared to who-knows-where, I have no idea how to proceed from here.

"As long as Kazuki Hoshino is your enemy, then you've made an enemy of me as well. And I can never die."

I remember what Haruaki once said to Maria. It seems like so long ago that I'm not sure I'm remembering word for word, though.

Yeah, I have to make sure I get Haruaki's help in this.

"Hey, is it okay if we pick up from where we left off earlier?" The shift is a little sudden, so Haruaki gives me a blank look at first, but then he nods with a smile. "So I was saying I figured out what to do next, right? I'll pick up from there."

I look Haruaki in the eyes and make my defiant declaration.

"I'm going to take down the Rejecting Classroom."

His eyes widen at the force in my voice.

"Uh… I'm pretty sure I told you that, in the Rejecting Classroom, we would live on with no harm done as long as we were oblivious."

"You did. But I can't do it. I can't ignore the idea that we could be trapped inside an endlessly looping world where it's impossible to progress even a single step forward."

"Why?"

"Because the truth is…I already know we are."

It's possible I could have lived out my days here trouble-free as long as I forgot about the Rejecting Classroom.

But I already know. I know that our lives here are all one huge lie.

There's no way I can ignore that.

Maybe it's selfish, but I feel it's not only the right thing to do, but also the only thing I can do.

"…I don't really get why, but you must have a good reason if you're sticking to your guns like this, right?"

The puzzlement in Haruaki's query is sincere.

A reason…? Why exactly am I clinging so fiercely to the normalcy of my daily life? I give it some thought. There's no denying that my attachment to the mundaneness of my existence probably borders on the abnormal.

Haruaki mutters, "It's like it's a matter of life and death to you."

Yeah, that's it. He hit it right on the nose. The reason couldn't be any simpler.

"It has to do with the reason why we live."

Haruaki's eyes widen, as if he didn't expect that sort of answer.

"The reason we live? And what is that? What do you mean?"

"I can't really explain it... Okay, say you had a test you didn't study for at all but still managed to ace. You wouldn't be that happy, would you? It wouldn't be the same as studying your brains out for a good score and then succeeding, right?"

"Sure. I know the things you have to work for are more important than the ones you get with little or no effort, even though the actual value might be the same."

"I believe that's what life is—that process of pursuing something. I don't think it's crazy at all. Everyone dies someday. The end result is always death. That's why going after the results alone is so scary to me."

"All people do die someday, that's true."

"If the place where we are now is that Rejecting Classroom where everything becomes null and void, I can't allow things to stay as they are. No way. I have to stay in the normal world if I'm going to protect the reason I live. That's why I despise the existence of these Boxes that run against normal life."

Haruaki listens to my full-on rant as if it's the most interesting thing in the world.

Maybe I didn't need to say all of that. After all, Haruaki would most likely offer his help unconditionally either way.

"So how about it? Will you help me?"

My friend's thumb shoots up without a moment's hesitation.

At Haruaki's suggestion, I ask Daiya and Kokone to hear me out and join us in our cause. The five of us are gathered around the bed in a room at the same ritzy hotel Maria and I went to before.

We lay out the situation to Kokone and Daiya.

I thought Maria might consider it a waste of time to explain everything to the others, but other than adding a few things here and there, she generally refrains from interrupting. Maybe she's hoping to hear a fresh perspective on our dilemma.

"Let's see... So Kasumi isn't actually Kasumi. She's someone named Aya Otonashi, and the real Kasumi is the 'owner' who made this 'Rejecting Classroom,' only now no one knows where she went, so Kazu here is asking us all to come up with a battle plan... It doesn't make any sense! How am I supposed to understand any of that?"

Kokone flops down sideways on the bed.

"Ahh, this is super comfy!" she says.

"Nobody asked what you thought of the mattress."

"I know that!" She lashes out at my little jest.

Even though she's playing around, I'm pretty sure her mind is actually hard at work thinking about what she's just heard.

"I have a few questions..." Daiya cuts in to the conversation. "If we are inside the Rejecting Classroom, then the accident you claim is unavoidable should happen like it always does, right?"

"Most likely."

Maria is the first to respond.

Uh, is Daiya actually taking this seriously?

"What's with that stupid look on your face, Kazu? You some fish in a pond flapping its mouth trying to get some food?"

"Uh, no, it's just that I'm surprised you believed what we told you about the Rejecting Classroom so easily."

"You think I believe that crap?" Daiya angrily spits out the words.

"Uh... Wha...?"

"I thought maybe you were the only one who lost your mind, but now even Mogi is talking crazy. There may be some extenuating circumstances driving you to do all this, but it's too much of a pain to think of what those could be. So I'm taking your story of the Rejecting Classroom at face value and putting my doubts on hold for now."

I take that to be Daiya's long-winded way of saying he's gonna help.

Haruaki has something to add.

"So, Daiyan. You said the accident might take place as always. What then?"

"Yeah, so if the accident occurs just as before, who will be the victim if Mogi isn't here anymore?"

"I...think it might be me, since I've been forced into her position in all this. The natural conclusion is that I will end up taking on her role in the accident, too."

Haruaki asks a question. "Was it always Kasumi who was struck?"

"No. Sometimes the people who tried to save Mogi would get hit, too. There was me, Kazuki, and even you when you tried to save me after I saved Mogi. That last one happened not just once but several hundred times."

"Whoa! Really? That number doesn't even seem possible. Oh, wait, never mind. I'm sure the same person in the same situation would take the same action in most cases."

"What's more, in nearly every instance at the start of the day, you told me how much you loved me," said Maria with an exasperated look on her face.

"I put my body on the line for the woman I loved? Awesome! I didn't know I was so cool!"

"To be perfectly honest, you were a bit of a nuisance."

"H-how could you...?"

"Try putting yourself in my shoes. How awful would you feel if you had to witness someone who had fallen in love with you die in your place? Your actions brought the arrogance of my quest to obtain the Box into sharp relief. Nothing else came so close to breaking my heart."

"Hmm..."

Haruaki scowls.

He looks like he still doesn't think his actions were entirely wrong, so I doubt he's sorry.

"By the way, how many times did I tell you I loved you?"

"Exactly three thousand."

"I didn't know I was so passionate..."

"That also means you got turned down three thousand times! That must be a new world record! But don't worry, Haru; there's something kinda cute about being such a loser!"

"Shut up, Kiri!!"

Those two crack me up.

"Mogi—no…I'll call you Otonashi for now. So, Otonashi, why do you think Mogi went to the site of the accident each time even though she knew what was going to happen there?" Daiya asks.

Maria's brows knit as she responds.

"The rules of the Rejecting Classroom most likely forced her to do so. I'm sure you've already figured this out, Oomine, but I tried to prevent the accident countless times."

"There's no reason to think she was okay with being run down by a truck when this all started. It's easier to assume things just worked out that way for her in the end. I still wouldn't choose to let myself get hit, though."

"Hey, why are you guys talking about the accident? I thought we couldn't solve any of this unless we find Kasumi."

Kokone tilts her head as she returns to the conversation. Daiya looks annoyed as he glances in her direction.

"Will someone please shut off the human noise generator?"

"Ha-ha-ha. Too bad you weren't the one who got splattered by that truck twenty thousand times, Daiya. ☆"

"Let me ask you, then, Kiri. How exactly do you propose we go about finding Mogi?"

"Well…I don't know. What, do you have some great idea, Daiya?"

"No."

"Huh. And to think you go around riding your high horse and calling me a noise generator. Hey, I know—why don't you change your last name to Highhorse? Daiya Highhorse. Wow, it's a perfect fit!"

"I'm not the only one without any ideas. None of the others know what to do either. Am I wrong?"

Haruaki and I look at each other. Yeah, he pretty much has it right. With that out of the way, Daiya plunges straight into his argument.

"What this illustrates is why we need to explore other avenues to solving this situation. I focused on the truck accident because it's clearly something of note within the cycle of repetition. This is clearly a logical deduction. I'm pretty sure even the human BS generator over there can understand that."

"Grr..."

Kokone grits her teeth in frustration at Daiya's jab.

"At any rate, stopping the accident could create a new development. It's worth giving it a shot, if there might be something there. That's what you want to say, right, Daiyan?" Haruaki sums up the argument.

Daiya nods. "Correct. But there's no point if the accident can't be stopped."

"No," Maria disagrees. "It might still be worth trying. There was a limit to what I could do working alone, but with this many people, we just might be able to put a stop to it."

"Will it matter if we have more people? If you multiply anything by zero, you're still gonna get zero. That's what it means to be impossible, right?" retorted Daiya.

"I understand what you're getting at, but I still see a few possibilities there. For one thing, the conditions now are different than they were before. I am Aya Otonashi, not Mogi, so the probability could now be something other than zero. If that's the case, then bringing more people onboard and bumping up our chances isn't a mistake, at the very least."

Daiya crosses his arms in thought for a moment before giving a slight nod and saying, "You may be right."

"All right! Now we know where to start! Let's stop that truck! Any objections?"

No one voices any dissent with Haruaki's roundup.

I think we might be onto something here.

It's early in the morning, an hour before the accident usually takes place. We all stand under our umbrellas at the intersection where it goes down.

Haruaki and I have been assigned to the task of helping Maria in the end. Both of us asked for this part, though it'll undoubtedly be dangerous if the wreck actually takes place.

Maria will find the truck that caused the accident and hijack it.

Having her behind the wheel gives her the lowest chance of getting hit by it, Maria claimed.

I'm nervous. There's no margin for failure. I couldn't sleep a wink last night. I was so anxious I spent several hours on the phone with Maria reviewing the plan.

I look at Haruaki next to me.

Unlike me, he doesn't seem tense at all. The look on his face is the same as ever. It's the expression Haruaki has always had during the entirety of our stay in the Rejecting Classroom.

This time, we may be able to destroy the classroom, *regardless of whether or not the accident takes place.*

"Hey, Haruaki. There's something I want to talk to you about while we wait. Is that cool?"

"What're you even asking for? Of course it's okay!"

The sound of the raindrops hitting my umbrella causes me to look up at the stormy sky.

"It's about Mogi."

"About Kasumi? You mean the original and not the Otonashi version here with us now?"

I nod.

"I don't think I told you about how Mogi killed me."

Haruaki frowns. "Damn. Must've been harsh."

The reason I didn't tell him wasn't that I was trying to hide it. I simply wasn't able to remember the events until after we figured out Mogi was the owner. Remembering who the owner was seemed to have unlocked all my other memories of the previous time.

"Mogi killed me, Maria, Kokone, and most likely you, too."

"...She killed me? Kasumi did? Why? What would she do that for?"

"She was kicking you all out. The Rejecting Classroom is a world where everything gets reset to its original state like it never even happened. If someone gets killed, that will be reset, too. But it seems Mogi has the ability to 'reject' people from the classroom if she kills them herself. My theory is that she does it when she truly doesn't want to see someone anymore."

Haruaki nods, his expression grave. I've explained the nature of rejection to him before, how it removes any means of remembering that person.

"I can't believe Kasumi did all that... But, well, I guess that's what happens to a person after experiencing almost thirty thousand loops in this place. It's not impossible that'd be the result."

"Do you really think so?" I ask.

"Yeah. It might be hard to imagine, but anyone would lose their mind if they were stuck in the same place for so long."

"Yeah, I can see that. But just because you lose your mind doesn't mean you start killing people. It isn't the kind of idea that normally pops into people's heads."

"Really? Maybe that's just your own values influencing how you see things."

He may be right, but I still don't buy it. Those murders only became an effective means of rejection because of her guilt. I can't believe Mogi would be able to come up with the idea of performing such atrocious acts on her own.

"...You opened your heart to Maria three thousand times and got hit by the truck several hundred of those, right?"

"So I hear. I have no way of knowing for sure, though."

"Right. But all of those actions ended up hurting Maria in the end, correct?"

Haruaki smiles bitterly as he speaks.

"Yeah, but that wasn't my intention."

"So why do you think Maria suffered so much? Because so much repetition lends power to words and ideas, even if they're completely ridiculous and untrue. Let's say you think you're a handsome guy. Your confidence is going to take a big hit if you're told you're ugly ten thousand times, even if the people were joking."

"Sure."

"It's the same with Maria. After you professed your love to her three thousand times, she couldn't help but acknowledge your existence.

This is Maria we're talking about here. Even she must have felt something when you said she was your enemy."

"As long as Kazuki Hoshino is your enemy, then you've made an enemy of me as well. And I can never die."

I can't help remembering those words again.

"...Huh? Are you saying I finally flipped her switch?"

I laugh off Haruaki's joke.

"So what if someone suggested murdering people to Mogi a thousand times? She was on the brink of insanity and didn't have anyone else to rely on, so she might have actually been so desperate that it began to sound like a good idea."

Haruaki agrees.

"That would definitely be a rough spot to be in. It could be possible. The person suggesting murder would be a part of the stagnant world, so their actions and beliefs would never change. They'd probably even repeat themselves verbatim. If they said it even once, they could've said it a thousand times."

"That's true, but that wouldn't make it a problem so much as something like the accident. What I mean is..."

I finally shift my gaze away from the rainy weather.

"What if someone was intentionally doing and saying things to put her on that course?"

I fix Haruaki with a hard look.

My sudden scrutiny doesn't seem to bother him in the slightest.

"Huh? But that shouldn't be possible, right?"

The look on his face is still the same as ever.

"That's not true. Maria and I could have done it if we tried. You see what I'm saying? *It would be possible if someone persuaded Mogi while pretending to have lost their memories.*"

Haruaki quietly listens to my idea without offering any argument.

"I always thought that being able to remember gave us an unconditional advantage. You'd think that the more information you have, the better, right? That's not necessarily true, however. Retaining our memories can actually leave us open to repeated attacks from people who don't remember anything, or people who are acting like they don't. Meanwhile, the people who don't keep a grip on their memories are safe. From there, they can launch assaults on those of us at the front lines."

I experienced something like this when the person I loved told me to "wait until tomorrow," even though she wasn't in the memory-free safe zone.

"Suppose there was someone who was committing this type of mental warfare on Mogi from a safe position. They'd be well aware she was suffering, observing her to make sure she didn't secure some means of escape and preparing an answer for her in the form of murder. If that were the case..."

"If that were the case, then you could argue that person manipulated Mogi and was an accomplice to the murders in an abstract sense."

Haruaki speaks in an off-hand manner.

I don't dispute his line of thinking.

"Mogi might not be the only target of these attacks."

"Which means?"

"Mogi wasn't the only one at the forefront of all this. Maria and I were there, too. It all depends on what their end purpose was, but it's possible they also tried to manipulate Maria and me. Maybe they've already influenced us a bit."

"*You want to try killing me?*"

I remember these words someone said to me before.

I didn't hear them only once; I'm sure of it. I heard them multiple times, until they clung to my mind like a curse.

That isn't all. I was also shown dead bodies.

Maria received confessions of love, became a casualty herself in place of others, and was viewed with hostility.

My memories aren't complete, but I can at least recall that much. There are probably even more detailed traps I never noticed.

We're under constant attack by someone in a safe, risk-free position. If things don't go as that person wishes, they can keep trying over and over until they get the results they want.

"If we've been moving according to that person's designs even slightly, then that could mean..."

I swallow hard.

"...what we're doing now could all be part of their plans."

Haruaki has gone quiet. His umbrella hides his face from me.

The silence grows, but the rain seems oddly loud. I hear a small voice.

At first, I wonder what he's saying, but when I listen closely, I realize it's stifled laughter.

Haruaki moves aside his umbrella to show me his face.

His eyes are full of loathing for me, the corners of his mouth twisted upward in a smile.

"C'mon, Hosshi. What's up with that joke—sorry, 'epic theory'—of yours? None of that's even possible. People don't behave as expected. You know that, right? You definitely had some interesting ideas there, but you were so serious about it all I honestly didn't know whether to laugh. But that thought was kinda funny by itself, so I laughed anyway."

"Yeah, I guess it was a bit long-winded and hard to understand."

"...Long-winded? No, it's more about how you don't have the slightest clue what this mystery attacker is even trying to accomplish. No matter what their goal is, there has to be an easier way of doing things."

Haruaki still sounds so cheerful.

"Yeah, I don't know what motivates them. That's why I was going to ask you."

"...Me?"

There's no turning back if I continue.

"Haruaki..."

But I have no intention of doing that.

"Why have you forced us down this path?"

No response.

Haruaki's face is hidden behind his umbrella again.

He doesn't say anything. He probably doesn't feel like it.

"I forget exactly how, but you and I became friends not long after I came to this school, and then you also introduced me to Kokone and Daiya. If it weren't for you, my school life would've been a little less interesting. I owe so much to you."

I have no choice but to keep talking.

"We haven't even been friends for a year yet."

"So you're saying that's why none of this is strange?"

I shake my head. Not that Haruaki can see it.

"There are a lot of things I don't know, but there are also plenty of things I do. And there's one thing I can say for certain."

It's time to lay it all out.

"Haruaki Usui would never be able to drive us all to the brink like this."

I can see his face again.

He's looking at me, his eyes open wide.

"So..."

Finally, I say it.

"So...*who are you?*"

"You're being evasive! I don't buy it! Wait, don't tell me you're serious?! You lucky bastard! Kasumi's even cuter than usual these days, too!"

Haruaki said it so casually not long ago.

That's when I first noticed something was wrong.

The Rejecting Classroom has certain rules. No one around Mogi will notice any changes she undergoes. They won't even notice if Aya Otonashi takes her place. That's what forced me to ask why.

Why was Haruaki able to say that Mogi looked *even cuter than usual*?

That's not the only thing.

Haruaki was rejected.

Even I forgot about him. But somehow, *I was able to remember later.*

I chalked it up to the fact that he was my best friend. Still, why could I remember only him and none of the other people who had been rejected?

It was just a theory, but what if I didn't forget Haruaki completely because *someone else was inhabiting his body*?

The theory's full of holes and nowhere near strong enough to be decisive proof, but none of that matters anymore.

I've remembered.

I've dredged up a memory that was never meant to return.

"Do you have a wish?"

"This Box can grant any wish, no matter what it may be."

Those were the words of that figure that looked like anyone and no one.

"Tell me what you want."

I prepare to say the name, the name that I forgot for so long. The name of the being that gives away the Boxes.

And that name is…

"O."

The moment the word leaves my lips, Haruaki vanishes from his own face.

"Heh-heh."

His features don't transform; it's just that there's no trace of him left in that grinning visage. It's like an imposter draped in Haruaki's skin.

At last, the phantom we've all been pursuing for so long has been revealed.

O.

"Dammit. No one but the actual owner of the Box is supposed to know that name. That's odd."

"You got a bit careless with those slips of the tongue back there."

"Careless?"

O snickers as if what I said is truly hilarious.

"Not a single thing I've done has been careless. You're the strange one, for being able to find me with so little to go on."

"Am I?"

"Then are you saying that whenever someone isn't behaving as they should be, you assume they're possessed or someone else entirely?"

That definitely isn't true. No matter how strangely someone is acting, the idea that they're someone else is far too outlandish and implausible.

"Either way, you've found me. That means you know about my existence as the motivating force behind everything going on here. No one is supposed to be able to remember me."

"If so, then why do I remember?"

"Why indeed? It's truly a mystery to me. Perhaps the presence of Aya Otonashi has something to do with it. Either way, my existence is such that you can't simply learn about it from others," O blithely informs me, not realizing that I couldn't care less. "…Oh, that's right—you asked what I wanted. I'll tell you. It's not like I'm trying to hide it. *All I wanted was to observe you up close.*"

Those words trigger a certain sensation within me.

Yeah, there it is again.

The same strange discomfort I felt the first time I met O returns.

What is it? What is this emotion?

"...I'm afraid I don't understand. What would make you drive Mogi to do such things?"

"What motivated me to manipulate the owner? I told you that all this happened because I wanted to observe you, but maybe I need to break things down into simpler terms."

O begins speaking with great relish.

"I wanted to see how you would react to another person's Box. When I granted Kasumi Mogi's wish to redo the past, I was unexpectedly pleased for a moment. After all, it was an opportunity for me to see you exposed to the effects of a Box for an extended period of time. However, I soon realized my joy was misplaced, the reason being that I naturally wanted to observe as wide a variety of situations as possible. Unfortunately, this Box you all call the Rejecting Classroom is incapable of producing other patterns. Everyone followed the same path of behavior, and you were no exception. It didn't matter that Kasumi Mogi and Aya Otonashi were able to retain their memories. As long as you, the crucial element, couldn't hold on to yours, none of this would be of any interest to me at all."

My discomfort has grown to the point that I wrap my arms around myself to keep it at bay.

"So I decided to take a more hands-on approach. I subbed myself in for Haruaki Usui, who was in a perfect position to influence the three of you. Using Haruaki Usui, Aya Otonashi, and Kasumi Mogi, I could make you keep ahold of your memories and set the stage to my liking. The payoff for my efforts was the chance to watch you in fine form."

"Which means you're the one who set things up so Mogi would kill me?"

"Yes, because I wanted to see how you would react on the verge of being murdered by the one you love."

Mogi suffered for so, so long, just for that?

"I should also point out that you only harbored that love for Kasumi Mogi because I induced it in you."

"Wha—?"

My love was contrived...?

"Ohhh? And here I was certain you'd be well aware of that by now. But now I see it must have escaped your notice. Heh-heh... It's moments like these that make being up close and personal worth it. Truthfully, I could watch you just as easily from outside of the Box, but if I weren't in here with you, I'd most likely miss out on these amazing little reactions. Observing something from outside the Box makes it seem so distant. It's troublesome, like peering down from space at something on Earth using a high-powered telephoto lens. I can definitely see everything, but it's not easy to focus on minute details. Perhaps it was a fortuitous side effect, but I've found observing you firsthand as Haruaki Usui to be truly enjoyable."

I've finally identified the horrible feeling I've borne for so long.

Fear.

I've experienced it before, of course, but this is a terror of an entirely different form, to the point that I can't even grasp it.

"So, Kazuki Hoshino, what are you going to do now?"

I can't form words.

Now that I'm aware of own fear, my mouth is sealed shut.

"Did you really think uncovering my presence within Haruaki Usui would solve everything? If I were human and a murderer, all you would need to do is hand me over to the police. That in itself would be one kind of resolution. But that isn't going to work here, is it? Your goal is to restore things to normal. Just speaking with me like this isn't going to solve anything."

I'm in danger. Encountering O has become the greatest threat of them all.

"Therein lies the reason I didn't hide my identity as Haruaki Usui any more than I needed to. Yes, I took possession of the Box from its owner, Kasumi Mogi. I can even present it to you here. But that won't be necessary. I don't have to give you the Box simply because you recalled that I exist. And you certainly don't have the ability to force me to do so, either."

O is interested in me. But it's the sort of attention reserved for the subject of an experiment, nothing more, nothing less. I have no idea how to deal with someone who treats me this way.

So…

"Yup, you're right about that."

Of course, I'm not the one who could pull off such an irreverent retort.

"He doesn't have the ability on his own."

O looks at me as if searching for the source of the voice. He's right to do so, since it's inside my bag.

A truck's horn blares. Soon after comes the roar of an engine, and before long, we can see the large vehicle approaching. O watches it with the slightest bit of consternation. It's the same semitruck we're sick of seeing, and now it's barreling toward us.

Maria sits in the driver's seat.

"I was hoping I'd get to meet you, O."

She's speaking from the cell phone that's been turned on inside my schoolbag this whole time.

The truck approaches, yet neither of us moves. I hear the screech of the emergency brake. The rain is making it difficult to slow down, as expected. The semi is still bearing down on us. Still, O never takes even a single step back. Watching him, I can't move, either, nor can I stop myself from closing my eyes.

The sound of the brake fades.

I open my eyes again to see the truck right before them in the most literal sense.

O lets slip a faint smile and turns toward the driver's seat.

"And just what was the point of that silly display?"

"Just my way of welcoming you to the party. How fortunate you didn't get run over like Mogi."

I can hear Maria's voice coming from both my bag and in front of me.

She steps down from the truck, removing her headset and ending the phone call.

Maria stands before us, with no concern for the rain, and fixes her gaze upon O.

"So you were listening in on our conversation the whole time. I guess that means you were never interested in my strategy to begin with. Too bad. I had hoped to see Kazuki Hoshino's disappointment in its outcome."

"I was listening carefully when you detailed your plan, but Kazuki was the one who figured out who you really were and kept you busy."

It wasn't my intent to do that. I just didn't know when to tell her what I had figured out.

I did choose the timing for when I would get Haruaki's cooperation and have this conversation, however.

"It worked out perfectly, thanks to him. If I had been here, you might have continued to play innocent."

"So you went to the trouble of stealing the truck to make sure I knew you wouldn't be nearby. I applaud your hard work. Still, I can't help but wonder why you think I would try to maintain my cover if you were here. You may be a Box, but don't think that means you can actually do something about this situation."

"Oh, you didn't know? All my efforts must have gone to waste. Let me ask you this: Are you familiar with my Misbegotten Happiness?"

"Yes, of course I am. I also know that it could never have even the slightest effect on me."

"Heh-heh, your inhuman nature keeps you from truly understanding us, I see. Maybe this will help. I am prepared to do whatever it takes to get rid of you."

O's expression becomes a thin smile. "All you can do is trap other people in your Box. What makes you think you could ever do anything to me?"

"You still haven't figured out why I chose Kazuki, have you?"

Hearing my name brings me back into focus. O regards me with a gaze that is probably meant to be gentle but is actually bloodcurdling. It's like how you size up a piece of pork when you're considering how to cook it.

"...I see."

O smiles.

Maria levels an angry glare at O as she continues.

"Looks like you get it now. Kazuki has the ability to use Boxes. He may even be able to make use of my Box, Misbegotten Happiness. If he did, I'm sure he would wish for normal life to carry on. He would wish for it to happen *free from things that disrupt it, like the Boxes and you.*"

This is the part where O should be fighting back. Instead, the being's eyes merely lower sadly, without a trace of being overwhelmed, surprised, or even frustrated.

"I guess you never change, do you?"

Those are O's only words for Maria, despite the fact that she has prevailed after 27,755 loops in the Rejecting Classroom.

"Don't you know that if you get rid of me, you, as an inferior Box, will also disappear?"

Maria remains unfazed by O's words.

"I've known that all along."

"I'm sure you have." O still looks sad and seems perfectly unconcerned about the looming prospect of disappearing forever. "You still can't live for yourself, can you? You're only capable of acting on behalf of others. It must be such a miserable existence. I pity you. I truly do."

"Your pity isn't worth fish food."

"At first I found those rare aspects of your existence intriguing, but now I couldn't care less. A human without desires is nothing more than a machine, about as fit a subject for observation as a vacuum cleaner. Nothing could possibly bore me more."

Maria clenches her jaw in anger at O's remarks. I can understand why. She's declared this thing her enemy, yet all O has for her is dismissal and even sympathy.

"Fine," O says. "I don't particularly relish the idea of vanishing, either. Let's make a deal. I'll hand over the Box, and in return, you let me go. Does that sound fair?"

"…Hmph. Even in the face of annihilation, your bargaining point is still so selfish."

"You should be thankful I'm playing along with your little threat, though you have such a poor chance of actually seeing it through. There's no guarantee Kazuki Hoshino will use your Box as you intend, and even if he does, it's unlikely I'll disappear as you claim. I'm merely making this unnecessary concession as a token of respect for Kazuki deducing my presence."

"You're one to talk about concessions. All you're giving Kazuki is the dilapidated cage you've had him trapped in this entire time. You can make new enclosures whenever you want. I'm sure you were probably almost through with him anyway, about to toss him aside and replace him with your next toy."

"I'll leave that up to your imagination."

"Hmph… Kazuki, are you fine with this?"

Maria asks me for confirmation. I nod. I'm fine with anything as long as it does away with the Rejecting Classroom.

"Kazuki Hoshino, may I offer you a piece of advice?"

O is speaking to me.

"You are a human who doesn't wish for change. However, most owners find they do desire change once they obtain a Box. They want something. They want to become something. They want to get rid of something. They try to make these longings into reality. That means you'll inevitably come into conflict with your own nature as an owner."

I'm unsure of the intent behind the revelation, and my face tightens.

O observes me with great interest.

"Kazuki Hoshino, do you think of yourself as different?"

Why ask me that?

"…I think I'm normal."

"I see. Well, I'm afraid I have to tell you that you are not. But don't trouble your head if you find that unpleasant. The window of time when people can afford to be unique isn't that long. Such people are inevitably either cast by the wayside or hammered in the mold of society until they are no longer special. So relax. I'm sure you fall into the latter category."

O's smile remains in place the whole time.

"That's why you really are so unfortunate."

The words seem to bring this entity such pleasure.

"You've learned about the existence of these little ways of breaking the rules, after all. Now, whenever you encounter a situation that fills you with regret, you'll think, 'If only I had a Box…' No matter how much you shake your head and try to forget they exist, sadly for you, they always will. Boxes capable of granting any wish will always be there, and you'll never forget about the loopholes they offer.

Furthermore, as you live with this knowledge in your mind, there will inevitably come a time when you realize you need one."

O's expression never changes.

Yeah, I remember now...

I refused to take a Box. Not even that was enough, though. I was already bound by O's curse.

"You might not be different anymore when the time arrives that you need a Box. If so, you won't be able to use it, and the prospect of that dampens my spirits a bit. That's why from here on out, I'm going to interfere with you and those around you, just the slightest bit, so that you take a greater interest in using a Box."

What could I have done differently to avoid this burden?

In all likelihood, nothing.

I— No, all of us—were doomed from the moment we met O.

"Never fear, though. Even if you do cease to be unique, I will still provide you with a Box, should you need one. That's enough for me. All you would need to do then is let me hear your sound."

"...My sound?"

"Yes. I love the noises humans make above all others, but there is one particular tone that I find especially delightful. That's the sound I hope you would share with me. Hmm? And what is it, you ask? My tastes are pretty simple, so I'm sure you can probably guess, but I'll tell you anyway..."

O grins.

"It's the screeching of the human heart."

And with that said, the O resembling Haruaki Usui vanishes. A small box lies on the ground instead. Things begin changing of their own accord as soon as I reach for it.

The scenery around us immediately begins folding up with a loud *slam, slam*. I can see the walls of the world. The white wallpaper covering them splits and sprinkles to the floor as dust. The sickly sweetness clinging to my skin vanishes in favor of an oppressive dampness that I can only describe as unpleasant. My inner ears are thrown into disarray, and my head swims. It sounds like something breaking.

Something cracking. Something shattering. Someone shattering. This is despair. Undeniable despair.

The false scenery now gone, we find ourselves in a dark chamber. It's so cramped and claustrophobic that even half a day here would be enough to drive someone mad.

This is probably the inside of the Box.

In this cell-like room sits a girl grasping her knees tight, her face buried in them.

It's the girl I loved.

"...Mogi."

She slowly raises her head at my words.

"Oh..."

Those eyes that were once so lifeless now harbor a faint light.

"I can't believe this is happening. This is all too good to be true."

Tears run down her cheeks.

Something about this seems odd to me, and I soon realize why.

"...You really did come to save me."

So that's it.

She's finally learned to cry again.

"Mogi, I'm sorry, but I need to destroy the Rejecting Classroom."

"...I know." She nods tearfully.

"And I'm going to let that truck kill you."

"......I know." She wipes at her eyes. "I don't care if you destroy the Box. I don't care if you end my life. Just give me a moment. There's something I have to tell you."

Mogi searches inside her bag. She pulls something out but quickly moves her hand behind her back so I can't see.

Maria's eyes narrow.

"Mogi, don't tell me you still..."

Without a word of response to Maria, Mogi walks toward me, her hand still behind her back.

"Mogi, stop! It's too late for..."

"It's okay, Maria," I admonish her. I still can't see what Mogi is hiding, but I have a pretty good idea of what it might be.

Shooting me a questioning look, Maria steps around behind Mogi. Seeing what's in Mogi's hand, Maria gives an exhausted smile.

"Kazu, do you believe that some feelings never change?"

That's Mogi's question for me.

I know the answer right away, but it's not a kind one for her.

I can't bring myself to say it.

Maybe my reply would have been different had I not experienced the things I did within the Rejecting Classroom. But I have. I've experienced a world that lasted for almost an eternity. That's why I believe what I do about unchanging feelings...

"No, I don't."

Mogi listens carefully to my answer.

And then she smiles.

"You're right. I don't, either."

I suddenly look into her eyes. She seems to have expected this reaction, because she keeps smiling as she continues speaking.

"I thought my feelings for you would never change, but that wasn't true at all. My love ran out. I began to dislike you, to hate you and think you were a nuisance. I even tried to kill you. I realize now, though, that I depended on you. I clung to you for so, so long in the hope that you would release me from this place. I couldn't ignore you. I'm aware of how despicably selfish my feelings were. I had no other choice but to think of myself, though. I know what to call that emotion. I didn't believe feelings could never change, but I did believe in one single thing, for the entire time I was trapped inside the Rejecting Classroom."

Mogi gives me a weak, faltering embrace.

She presses the object she was hiding into my hand.

I can feel her lips trembling next to my ear.

"I loved you, Kazu."

Mogi's lips draw near mine but, just before they touch, stop.

Her lips remain there for moment before slowly drawing away, having never reached mine.

I almost ask her why she didn't do anything, but I decide against it.

I look down at what she gave me.

"Ah..."

There's the reason.

Having realized this, I bite my lip.

I was expecting something entirely different.

In my hand is an Umaibo.

Everything up to that point went as I thought it would. But this isn't my beloved corn potage flavor. This is teriyaki burger, the flavor I'm not particularly fond of. It's the one Mogi was originally supposed to give me.

Why was her embrace so timid? Why didn't she actually kiss me?

I know why. This isn't a profession of love from the Kasumi Mogi of the Rejecting Classroom, the girl who opened her heart to me and even kissed me so many times before.

This Mogi could never refer to me by anything other than my last name.

This is the first time she told me how she felt, before she entered the Rejecting Classroom.

I want to do March 2 over again.

Mogi has just reenacted my greatest regret from that day, the one thing I wanted to redo.

Am I supposed to give the same reply I did on the real March 2…?

I look at Mogi.

She's smiling gently, waiting for the response she knows so well.

"I…"

I can't.

I don't want to say those words.

I actually loved Mogi, after all. O may have manipulated me to have them, but the feelings themselves were not false.

Why am I only allowed to say things that bring pain to Mogi?

The answer is plain to see.

I've rejected this Box. I've rejected Mogi's wish. I'm going to make her into a body lying on the road. I have no right to say anything kind to her.

My mouth opens.

It's still difficult to summon the answer. As I stand there with my mouth opening and closing, wavering in indecision, I'm startled at the taste of a salty liquid running into my mouth.

These are the only words left to me:

"Wait until tomorrow."

*   *   *

Mogi lowers her eyes sadly.

I have no reason to expect her not to be hurt. But her expression soon changes.

"Thank you."

She says that with a smile.

Truly, one from the bottom of her heart.

Yeah, I remember that smile at last.

I saw it once during a conversation with her.

The one where I realized I was in love with her—where this love I'm about to lose first blossomed.

It's a precious memory.

"Hoshino, will you call me Kasumi?"

"Uh, wh-why do you ask that all of a sudden?"

"It may seem out of the blue to you, but I've wanted to ask you that for a long time."

"Oh…I see."

"So…will you do it?"

"S-sure…"

"A-and, oh, by the way…c-can I call you Kazu?"

"Um…sure. I don't mind."

"Okay, try saying it."

"…Kasumi."

"…One more time."

"Kasumi."

"…Thank you."

"Ah…! Wh-why're you crying…?!"

"Oh, am I?"

"Y-yeah, you are…"

"Well…it must be because I'm so happy, Kazu."

And then *Kasumi* smiled, her eyes still full of tears.

I had never seen a smile like that before, a smile so genuinely full of happiness.

It was the first time I ever made someone elated. The experience was so new, and it made me unbelievably happy as well.

Bringing joy to others is joy itself.

I was delighted to learn this about myself, and the girl who taught me this became very special to me.

I might be the simplest person out there, but there's no denying that one smile changed my entire existence.

But now I'm getting ready to erase that memory.

I'm going to obliterate this new emotion.

It's too horrible. Why does something like this have to await me at the very end? Asking me to destroy it with my own hands is too cruel.

Regardless, I've already chosen this path.

I set myself on it long, long ago.

The Rejecting Classroom can do away with all of this insanity in an instant, right?

"Maria, can I ask you for a favor?"

I'm hovering on the brink, and I need only a little push.

"Go for it."

"You must know what I'm about to do."

"Naturally. I've watched you more than anyone else in the world has."

"So what am I going to do? I want you to tell me."

Maria nods, her expression grave. I'm certain she understands why I'm asking this of her.

"You're going to destroy it."

Even at a time like this, Maria can't phrase things gently.

"You're going to destroy someone else's ill-chosen wish for your own sake. You will never, ever back down from this."

She's right. I believe this is the correct choice.

"That's why you're going to destroy the Box."

I nod at Maria's assertion.

I wipe away my tears using my entire left arm.

"That's exactly right."

I stand before one of the walls.

The ashen sides enclosing us are thin, as if made of paper. There's no more power left in this Box. It's just preserving my memories, keeping them from escaping for a bit longer.

I want to turn around and get one last look at Kasumi, but I have the feeling that's something I absolutely must not do.

I raise my left hand.

Then, to demolish this Box, Kasumi's wish, and my memories, I raise my right.

"Thank you. I knew you would be the one to free me from this place in the end, Kazu."

Stop it.

She shouldn't be grateful. I'm only tearing down this place, stomping her mistaken wish into oblivion.

I'm sorry.

Please forgive me for not being able to save you.

I ignore her words, but I'm thankful for them all the same.

That final smile gives me the faith in myself I need to do this.

"Aaaaaaaaahhhhh!!!"

Roaring as loud as I can, I hit the wall with all my might.

A terrific noise resounds through the wall, and it shatters like glass.

I can see Kasumi amid the shards raining down. We smile at each other happily.

The pieces fall, break, and turn to dust.

A white light shines in from outside the walls. Each time another section falls, the light devours the gloom. It washes over everything until I can see nothing apart from us.

Eventually, it's too bright to see at all.

Or so I thought. For some cruel reason, I can see Kasumi clearly, as she once was before all of this.

She's lying in the middle of the road, covered in blood. Her pain and suffering are so apparent that it's all I can do to keep from looking away. But she's smiling. She's trying with all her might to smile for me.

I open my mouth to speak.

"Good-bye."

★   ★   ★

The pure white light then claims us, and we vanish.

The radiance courses through me, violently searches out every last bit of my body, finding its way inside and consuming me. My organs, my blood, my heart, and my brain turn white. The light even finds its way into my memories, bleaching them as well. My memories that are false yet so precious at the same time, my new feelings, the words we just exchanged—it all fades.

All fades to white.

All fades to white.

All fades to white…

1st Time

"I'm Aya Otonashi. Pleased to meet you."

The transfer student smiles faintly.

Her beauty sends ripples through the other girls, and while you'd think the boys would be excited, too, they merely sit in shell-shocked silence.

I'm no different. I've never seen someone as attractive as her. I don't think I could look away even if I wanted to. Our eyes meet, and her gaze draws me in with no resistance. She seems used to the reaction, and she flashes me a quick smile as we look at each other.

I feel like my head is spinning.

I'm going to fall for her, even though I know it'll most likely never work out. She's way out of my league. It feels like she came out of another world. I probably sound a bit weak for putting it that way, but I'm pretty sure anyone would feel the same looking at her.

"Let me start by saying the answer is no."

The smile never leaves her face as she says all of this.

"I, Aya Otonashi, do not want you to be nice to me."

A hush falls over the classroom.

With just a few words, she has silenced the uproar among her classmates, almost as if she cast some sort of magic spell.

"Please don't think poorly of me. I would like to be friends with all of you, if I could. But I'm afraid that is impossible. Allow me to explain why..."

Her face grows melancholy, but she continues on in a faint voice.

"My existence as Aya Otonashi will never be anything more than an illusion."

I don't understand what she's trying to say, but something about her tone makes me swallow nervously.

"We were never meant to fit together. From our respective viewpoints, we are all simply dreams. The reason why is that I am a transfer student. We aren't acquainted, you don't know me, and we will always return to this state in the end. I must continue to avoid forming connections with others and never entertain any thoughts of bonds. I truly am nothing more than an illusion among you. However, I take pride in my identity as an illusion. It's also occasionally a source of pain for me. But I must accept it, for if I ever fail to do so, if the weight of being nothing more than a vision overwhelms me, then I will lose myself within this false world of repetitions."

I can't make heads or tails of what she's saying, but I can tell she's completely serious and not likely to stand for anyone making fun of her.

"I have abandoned my true name within this Box in order to become this illusion. I felt that using my real name would be a hindrance, repeatedly drawing me back to who I really am. If I fall victim to the false repetitions here, then I'm sure all of you will vanish, too."

Her tone intensifies.

"That is why I must persist as an illusion, as Aya Otonashi."

Ah, I get it. I don't completely understand it all, but it feels like she isn't actually Aya Otonashi yet. She's going to become Aya Otonashi from this point onward.

I'm sure it's against her will, and I'm sure it isn't something she wants.

But regardless, she still has to assume this identity.

"I'm not strong," she says bitterly. "There will be times when I want to complain and be weak. But if I ever do so in the course of what lies ahead, I will cease to be Aya Otonashi. So in order to ensure that doesn't happen, I am going to voice all my weakest thoughts right here and now. I..."

A coincidence. Yeah, it has to be a coincidence, but still, right when she starts speaking, she looks at me.

"I want someone to stand beside me."

Then she smiles at me.

"I will now introduce myself again."

When she speaks, it sounds like she's making the introduction to herself as much as to us.

"I am Aya Otonashi. I am pleased to meet you all, for the many times to come."

Aya Otonashi bows deeply to the class.

Unsure of what to do, no one in the class says a word.

That's why I start clapping.

The sound of my hands coming together resounds throughout the classroom.

Eventually, someone else joins me, and then someone follows our lead. Others join in, and the sound of the applause increases. Once we're all clapping, she finally raises her face to look at us.

She's no longer smiling.

She's standing bravely, facing straight ahead with her fists clenched tight.

The deep-blue sky is clearer than I ever thought possible.

I check the date as soon as I wake up. It's April 7. Today is April 7. I check the newspaper and TV just to make sure it really is April 7. I know there's no meaning in reconfirming it so many times, but ever since the day I became trapped inside the Rejecting Classroom, it's become the only way to put my mind at ease.

The events that took place within the Rejecting Classroom remain in my mind as information, but recalling those memories is like viewing pictures of me that were taken without my knowledge. The Box, Maria, O—I know who and what they all are, but they stir no emotions, no anger or sadness or anything inside me. I'm sure that's why I'm also slowly forgetting I was once in love. The memories are all so thin and tenuous that they're slipping through my fingers bit by bit.

I'm sure it's the same for Maria.

We were never meant to meet in the first place, so I'm certain we won't do so again now.

Anyway, today is April 7, the first day of school.

I'm now a second-year student.

My homeroom is on the third floor now instead of the fourth. Just being a little lower and farther to the west isn't going to change the scenery from the window much. But when I enter classroom 2-3, the atmosphere feels completely different, and my chest tightens with elation.

My eyes land on a printout lying on my teacher's desk, detailing the seating arrangements. I take a seat in the one assigned to me by the chart. I greet my new classmates with a gentle "Nice to meet you," which they return in kind. Yeah, this is going to be nice.

Another face enters the classroom.

When he spots me, he raises a hand in greeting.

"Wassup, Hosshi? Looks like we're in the same class again!"

He hasn't said anything strange, but all fifteen of the people in the room turn to look at us.

Yep, Haruaki is as loud as ever.

"...Hey, Haruaki."

"Huh, what's up?"

I regard him with a suspicious look. "Is it really you?"

"...Why're you looking at me like I could be some sort of fake? You think I have a twin brother or something? Maybe one of those super-famous manga out there has you convinced that all high school pitchers are twins!"

"...That's not it."

I guess it's going to be a while before I stop suspecting Haruaki...

"By the way, Hosshi, have you heard—?"

"Hey, it's Haru and Kazu!" A new voice cuts Haruaki off midsentence.

Kokone stands by the door of the classroom with Daiya next to her.

Did the two of them actually come to school together like friends? If I point that out, I'm sure I'll spend the rest of the day enduring Daiya's mental torture, so I keep my mouth shut.

"I felt my heart leap at the sound of a woman's voice, only to find out it was just Kiri. You really know how to take the wind out of a guy's sails!"

"What the hell type of reaction is that, Haru? Who do you think you are?"

"Yeah, well, I know you're a big fan of mine, but I really have to draw the line at you following me to another class, you know? That's all I was trying to say."

"Ha! Sounds like you're just trying to cover up the fact that you're madly in love with me. You're such a child. And while we're at it, maybe you should stop filling up your phone with recordings of my oh-so-cute voice?"

"Who the hell would do that?!"

"'Yes, Master!' ...C'mon, Haru, it's the perfect chance to add another clip to your adorable little collection! Here, I'll give you another. Maybe you'd like it if I said 'Welcome home, Master!' this time?"

I don't know what to make of their conversation, but I do know it's embarrassing, so I hope they'll stop soon.

"Ugh... Hey, Kazu, you don't have any firecrackers on you by chance, do you? I wanna light one up and throw it in Kiri's mouth so we can have some peace and quiet."

"Oh, look, it's Daiya. He must be jealous because I'm giving Haru here all my finest voice samples. Don't you worry, though. If you bow down and lick my shoes, I might just call you 'Big Brother' in my best little sister voice. Wow, I'm so nice!"

"Could I get you to say 'I'm sorry for ever being born'?"

...Here I am in a new class, yet nothing has changed at all.

Still, this is exactly what I wished for.

I'm sad that Mogi and Maria aren't here, but this is what I fought the Rejecting Classroom so hard to restore.

"...What're you grinning at by yourself over there, Kazu? You look like a creep."

Daiya brings everyone's attention to me.

"Ew, he's right! Kazu has a huge grin on his face. He must be having a little laugh to himself or is probably thinking something perverted. Yeah, I'll bet he's imagining what it'd be like to have a little fun with the girl sitting next to him."

"I'm not."

I shut that down right away. Kokone purses her lips.

"Whose seat is this, anyway? Someone I know? Someone cute?" Haruaki asks, even though he's sitting in said seat like he owns it. I know the person's name because I checked who would be sitting there out of curiosity while finding my own seat.

"Yeah, it's a cute girl."

"Really? Who?"

She has a desk here. That at least makes me happy. As long as she has a seat here, she can take it one day. Who knows? That seat may not be next to mine anymore by the time she makes it back, but that doesn't upset me.

I smile and say the name of the one assigned to the seat next to mine. *"It's Mogi."*

It was raining so hard, you could easily imagine it would never stop.

When I heard from Daiya that Mogi had been in an accident, I rushed to the hospital. There would be no school for me today. The place they brought her to wasn't in the city, so I took a taxi. For someone like me who loves the tranquility of normal life more than anything else, it was an almost unthinkable action.

I had no other choice, though. I had to know the outcome after all my struggles in the Rejecting Classroom.

I arrived at the hospital before anyone else, even Mogi's own family. Most people mistook me for her boyfriend, so I ended up waiting with her family until the surgery was completed.

The operation seemed to have been a success...at first. But Mogi didn't regain consciousness that day.

I wasn't allowed in the ICU, so it wasn't until she was moved to the general ward two days later that I was able to see her.

Looking at her lying on the bed like that was painful. The noise of the EKG and artificial respirator rattled my eardrums. Her arms and legs were restrained, and her face was a mess of bruises and scratches. The IV dripped fluids into her arm, which was now purple.

The sight of an injured friend in the hospital is enough to elicit tears in anyone. But I wasn't the one who wanted to cry. I couldn't, not in front of her. I held back my anguish and peered closely at her face.

Mogi looked at me. She seemed the slightest bit surprised, but the muscles of her face hadn't moved, so I couldn't be certain.

While I had heard from Mogi's family that she had regained consciousness, I had also been told that, perhaps due to the shock of the accident, she had yet to speak a single word.

Despite this, she struggled to open her mouth, as if she wanted to tell me something. I told her not to strain herself, but she kept trying anyway.

Her exhalations fogged up her oxygen mask, but eventually, she spoke her first words.

"I'm so happy. I'm alive after all."

I couldn't quite catch everything, but that's what I think she said.

With that off her chest, Mogi began to cry.

I wasn't sure where to look, and my gaze swam over the room before finally coming to rest on Mogi's tattered bag sitting next to her bed. It was open, and I could see a silver wrapper inside. I knew why it was there, so I reached in and pulled it out—a teriyaki burger–flavored Umaibo. The snack had lost its shape and was now just a bunch of crumbs inside the wrapper. As I ran my fingers over it, I realized I couldn't bear it anymore and started sobbing.

I didn't understand why then, of all times. I had memories of receiving this from Mogi in that other world, but I couldn't recall why she'd given it to me.

None of that made any difference to my tears, however.

I went on to visit Mogi many times in her room after she moved to the general ward. She always did her best to sound cheerful when she spoke to me.

"I had a really long dream while I was unconscious," Mogi said during one of my visits. It seemed she genuinely believed everything had taken place in a dream.

A thought suddenly popped into my head. In that world, nothing could alter Mogi's fate of being hit by that truck. At the same time, nothing could change the fact that she would survive. That could be why the Rejecting Classroom was never destroyed despite Mogi experiencing the accident so many times.

Mogi had survived, but she would apparently never use her legs again. She had taken a powerful blow to the back that injured her spinal cord. There was little to no chance it would ever recover.

I had no idea what the appropriate response was when I heard this news, so I stayed silent. Apparently concerned for my feelings, Mogi spoke instead.

"I thought maybe I would feel like I was better off dead if things ended up like this. You can understand why, right? I'll never walk on my own again. I'll never be able to just pop by the convenience store again if I feel like having some dessert. I'll always have to depend on other people or drag my wheelchair out to go by myself. That's a lot of work just for some sweets. It's horrible. But the funny thing is, none of that is enough to make me want to die. I wonder why. I truly, truly do."

…Because you're happy to be alive.

Mogi continued on, without a hint of gloom or false courage.

"I'll be fine. I won't give up on school, either. I'll make it back, no matter how long it takes. We may not be in the same year anymore when that day comes, but I'll still keep trying."

Mogi smiled and flexed her arm weakly.

I'm embarrassed to say that I cried in front of her that day. I was just so, so happy that her greatest wish had come true.

…Is there anything I can do?

I wanted to help however I could, truly. That's why I asked.

After saying it would probably sound a bit forward, Mogi made her request with a hint of flushed cheeks.

"I want you to leave a place open for me to return to. I want you to create somewhere I can belong again."

…Again? Did I make a place where Mogi belonged in the past?

"……I'm talking about that long dream."

After replying, she blushed for some reason and looked away.

I'm at our school entrance ceremony.

As I glance over at Haruaki where he sits yawning next to me in the gym, no longer able to feign interest in the principal's speech, something occurs to me.

"Now that I think about it, Haruaki, weren't you about to say something when I ran into you this morning?"

"Huh? …Oh yeah, oh yeah! I heard a rumor that one of the new students this year is really hot!" Haruaki slaps me on the shoulder and winks.

"Oh, I don't really care about that. She'll just be an underclassman anyway, so it's not like I'll have much chance to see her."

"Are you an idiot?! Just looking at pretty girls is enough to make a man happy!"

I don't want to believe this is how everyone sees things.

"So when did you hear that rumor, anyway? I mean, I haven't seen any of the new first-years before this ceremony today."

"That's the thing. I got the info straight from Daiyan."

"From Daiya?"

Now, that I just can't believe. I've never known Daiya to be one to talk about girls.

"You don't believe me, do you? Well, there's a good reason why only he would know. You've heard how Daiyan got only two questions wrong total for all subjects during his entrance exam, right?"

"Of course. He never lets anyone forget it, either. He says it was a new school record."

"Welp, I'm afraid to say that record didn't make it more than a year! Too bad, so sad, Daiyan!"

Haruaki could not look any more pleased as he delivers this revelation. There's really nothing anyone can do for this guy...though I have to admit I understand why he's so happy with Daiya's misfortune.

"Okay, so what does that have to do with why Daiya knows about this cute girl?"

"You aren't the sharpest, are you, Hosshi? This lovely lady got a perfect score in every subject and blew his record out of the water. One of the teachers apparently decided to tell Daiyan as the previous record holder. He even said the girl was so beautiful, she made a grown-up like him bashful."

That has to be an exaggeration. Why would the teacher be nervous? This girl wouldn't have even half his life experience.

The principal's speech ends while we're talking.

The teacher in charge of the ceremony takes the microphone.

"Thank you. And now we have an introduction from the representative of our new students this year..."

"Oh man, here she comes! The beauty everyone's talking about!"

Huh, she must be representative because she's top of the class.

Even I'm getting curious by now, so I scan the stage to see if I can spot her.

"Here is the representative for the new students, Maria Otonashi."

...Maria Otonashi?

I swear I've heard that name before. No way—that isn't possible. Besides, "Maria" was Aya Otonashi's nickname.

"Yes."

That voice sure does sound like Maria's, though.

Oh yeah, now it all makes sense.

"Even if you forget everything, at least remember this: My name is Maria."

Wow, I guess she was actually telling the truth.

...Wait. That means I was calling Maria by her first name the entire time...? Argh! Aaaaaahhh!

"...What're you turning red for, Hosshi?"

Maria takes the stage with more grace than anyone in the room. Having lived for longer than everyone here, her dignity is already palpable.

Just her turning to face the front is enough to set the students abuzz.

I know that face well.

It's the face of the girl who was beside me for so long.

Her uniform is brand-new.

Yeah, this is definitely out of the ordinary. I've never once thought of Maria as being younger than I am.

Maria casts her gaze over the crowd once she reaches the podium.

It stops on me for some reason, never wandering from there.

Then she smiles.

Simply put, my entire body goes numb.

Maria begins her speech, keeping her eyes on me the whole time.

The commanding tone of her voice brings the excited students to a hush.

"Hey, why does she keep looking this way? Oh, damn, what if she's fallen for me?!"

I hear Haruaki's joke, but I can't take my eyes off Maria, much less voice a response.

I watch her the whole time.

Maria does the same.

"This concludes the greeting from Maria Otonashi, the representative of the new students."

She steps down from the stage.

The moment she does, all the students go back to their previous level of commotion. Except, this time it isn't just the students—the teachers are getting in on it, too.

No one is more rattled than I am, though. I'm sure of that.

Maria is coming this way instead of returning to where she was standing previously.

Her force of presence is so strong that the students before her automatically clear a path without a single complaint. And she's following that path straight this way.

It's leading to me.

Why am I not surprised? It seems Maria still hasn't kicked all the habits she picked up in that other world. She never needed to think twice about her actions there, but things don't work that way here.

I can practically see my precious normal life falling apart around me.

All I can do is laugh.

"Ha-ha…"

What a pain.

Yeah, it'll be a huge pain, but…I won't think of it that way at all.

The last students standing between us move aside. Haruaki, too.

The entire area around me has emptied as if I'm in the eye of a storm. Maria stands directly before me in this little bubble of space.

I never thought I would see her again, but when I think about it, there's no reason to expect she wouldn't seek me out. She's on a mission to obtain a Box, after all, and with O targeting me, sticking close by is her best option.

Maria smiles.

She slowly parts her lips to speak.

"I think I made some declaration once saying I would always be beside you, no matter how much time passed, and it looks like that oath is still in effect."

With that said, she stands straight and introduces herself properly.

★   ★   ★

"*I am Maria Otonashi*. Pleased to meet you."

The new student bowed deeply, just as she once had so long ago.

And just as I had once done so long ago, I clapped my hands.

The sound of my hands coming together resounded through the gymnasium for a moment.

Then Haruaki, even though he didn't really get what was going on, began clapping where he stood next to me. Someone else joined in. The sound of the clapping grew louder, though no one really knew why. In the midst of this sea of applause, Maria raised her face to look at us all.

She was no longer smiling.

She stood bravely, facing straight ahead with her fists clenched tight.

AFTERWORD

Hello, this is Eiji Mikage.

Three years have passed since the release of my last book. If any of you out there were waiting for something new from me, I'm very sorry for the long delay. Also, thank you very much for not forgetting about me. Though there were times when the words didn't seem to flow as they should, I can assure you I never once gave up writing. The reason I didn't release any work for three years lies entirely in my own lack of ability.

I wrote this story with the intent of making it as entertaining as I possibly could. My stance on how I write novels also changed.

These changes made me very nervous. What if the things that made my work good disappeared? What if the readers who had supported me for so long felt betrayed? What if my work became lost amid all the other great stories out there?

Those were some of the anxieties I battled the whole time I was writing *The Empty Box and Zeroth Maria*.

But somewhere along the way, those fears vanished, all because I realized this story was undeniably mine.

I think this book turned out to be one where I can say "Just give it a shot" to people, whether they're fans of my previous work, readers who maybe didn't care for what I did before, or new readers who have never heard of me before this.

So how was it? Did you find it an enjoyable read? If your answer is yes, then I couldn't be any more pleased.

As it turns out, this fourth book of mine is the first to feature illustrations. I had thought adding cover art would change how readers viewed the book simply on a surface level, but I realized this was wrong once I received the rough drafts of the art in the mail. It was the sensation of finding out my characters weren't entirely mine any longer. They had escaped my dominion. The book was already pretty much done by the time I saw how my characters looked, so I can say there wasn't much reverse influence. I have no doubt, though, that the independence of these characters will have an impact on my work.

I look forward to seeing how it all plays out.

I received the support of a great many people in the process of writing this book. We're talking a whole new level of gratitude here. Thanks to all their cooperation, I was finally able to keenly feel that sense of completing a book for the first time.

The list of people I want to acknowledge may be a bit long, so please bear with me.

I would like to say thank you to the editors, proofreaders, designers, and members of all the other departments at ASCII Media Works.

Thank you to 415, who was kind enough to provide the illustrations for this book. I was a bit nervous, since this was my first time using illustrations, but as soon as I saw his work, all those fears were swept away. Now when I see art by 415, I grin and start coming up with all sorts of ideas.

Thank you to all my friends and coworkers at my part-time job who helped me grow along the way.

Thank you to my family, who watched over me when I just couldn't seem to put a book out.

Thank you to Yu Fujiwara, who cheered me on during the low points when I felt like I was at my most rotten.

To all my drinking buddies in Shinjuku: thank you for tossing ideas my way and keeping my spirits high.

Thank you to my manager, Kawamoto-san. I can safely say that without you this book would not exist. All joking aside, looking back on how I used to be, I'm surprised you stuck with me. You have helped me grow in many ways, not just related to this book here. I'm truly grateful.

And last but not least, thank you to all you readers out there holding this book in your hands now.

A book is complete only once it's read. It may sound forward to say you're a part of this novel, but let's just say you're an essential element. Nothing would please me more than to express my gratitude and return the favor by giving you at least a little entertainment.

I sincerely hope that we can keep this partnership going for some time to come.

Oh, and one last thing! Sorry the afterword was so boring!

Eiji Mikage